Waltham Fo███

Please return this item by the ████████ ███ may be
renewed unless requ███ ██ █████ ██████████

10 · 9 · 2019.		

Need to renew your books?
http://www.walthamforest.gov.uk/libraries or
Dial 0333 370 4700 for Callpoint – our 24/7 automated telephone renewal
line. You will need your library card number and your PIN. If you do not
know your PIN, contact your local library.

free REIN

Truth or Mare

by
Catherine Hapka

Based on the original TV series created by
Vicki Lutas and Anna McCleery

Scholastic Inc.

To everyone

who grabs the reins
of their own life

$\mathcal{E}$asy, Raven!" Zoe Phillips laughed as her horse tossed his head and snorted at some rustling leaves in the bushes beside the dirt road. "It's only a bird!"

"He's just feeling good." Zoe's best friend Jade rode up beside her with a smile. "We all are. It's such a gorgeous day!"

"Simply wonderful," shouted a voice from the back. It was Becky, Zoe's other best friend. Zoe had to agree with her friends. Back in Los Angeles, where she was from, everyone always talked about how perfect the weather was. But in Zoe's opinion, California couldn't hold a candle to this place—this island off the coast of England where her mother had grown up, and where Zoe had been living for over a year now. She missed California every day, but on days like this, it was a little harder to imagine living back there. And she had Raven to thank for being here . . .

She patted the big, black horse on the neck. Raven was so special to her. He'd taught her so much.

And her equally special friends, of course. Zoe glanced back at the rest of the group. Right behind her was Gaby, who had once been her rival and was now her friend . . . at least most of the time. She was a former foster kid who'd talked her way into a spot at the most prestigious riding school on the island, Holloway Academy. But after she'd been kicked out, she'd come to Bright Field Stables—and to Zoe's grandfather's house. Living with Gaby wasn't always easy, but it was definitely interesting!

Behind Gaby came three younger riders. There was Heather, whose mother was mayor of the island and who had recently received her own pony, Princess, as a birthday gift. Beside her was Winnie, Becky's biggest fan and a brand-new rider. Winnie had been bullied in the past and Bright Fields was her happy place. And finally there was Zoe's cousin Aaron who had spent some time on the island before. He was living back in California, but his mother had let him visit the island as a late birthday gift. Together, they were known as the Breakfast Club.

Bringing up the rear was Zoe's other best fr... Becky, who as usual was riding Bob, her stout, hairy Irish cob. At the moment, the reins were draped on Bob's neck, since Becky was using both hands to film the other riders with her sticker-encrusted phone.

Just then Jade looked back, too. "Becky!" she exclaimed. "Can't you keep at least *one* hand on the reins, for goodness' sake? Safety first, you know."

"Don't worry." Becky peered at the phone, shifting her viewfinder from the Breakfast Club over to Jade. "Bob knows where we're going. He's got a super sense of direction, practically a walking compass. Especially when he's heading toward food—oi, Bob, quit that!" She grabbed for the reins with one hand as Bob dove for a patch of grass beside the trail.

Jade rolled her eyes and Zoe laughed, hoping that her friends never changed. Jade was smart, sensible, and a lot of fun, but she liked to follow the rules. Becky believed in making up her own rules—in riding, in fashion, and in life—which was probably why she got along so well with the often mischievous Bob.

"Why are you recording us, anyway?" Gaby spoke up, glancing over her shoulder at Becky. "It's not as if we're doing anything exciting."

"Right." Zoe shrugged. "I mean, we already saved the wild herd and caught all the local criminals, right?"

Jade shot her a look. "Good thing Mia's not here," she said. "You shouldn't say things like that in front of her, you know."

"Of course I wouldn't!" Zoe protested.

That was true. But she felt a twinge of guilt for joking about it, anyway. Not so long ago, Mia's father had been caught cutting corners on the fancy new resort hotel he'd just built on another part of the island, which had resulted in tainted lake water that had made the local wild horse herd very sick. He'd been in prison ever since, awaiting trial. Mia was still coming to Bright Field Stables as often as ever, but she'd been pretty quiet, and had decided not to come along with the rest of the group today. Her best friend, Susie, had decided to stay with her back at the stables.

"Okay, so my question stands." Gaby shot another look at Becky. "Is what we're doing right now really worthy of inflicting on the Internet?"

That was just like her. If there was one thing Zoe had learned about Gaby, it was that she never gave up on something she wanted, whether that was the answer to a question or a coveted spot on the Under 18 UK Squad.

Zoe and Gaby had fought it out all through the

tryouts, and it had hurt when Gaby won the spot on the UK team in the end. Now Zoe had a chance to try out for the team back home in America, but was it really worth leaving her friends behind? Sometimes Zoe imagined what life would be like back in the States. She'd changed so much since she'd lived here. But maybe it would be fun!

Lost in thought, she tuned in just in time to hear Becky's response to Gaby. "I promised Alex I'd film today for him, since he couldn't come along." Becky sighed happily.

Zoe smiled at Jade, who grinned back. Both of them were thrilled about their friend's romance with Alex, a rider from Holloway. He was Becky's first boyfriend ever, and she was flinging herself into the relationship with her usual enthusiasm.

"Why couldn't he come today?" Winnie asked.

Becky shrugged. "I'm not sure, actually," she said, lowering her phone for a moment. "He texted that he had an appointment and he'd see me later. I figured that meant a trip to the dentist, but who knows. I suppose he'll fill me in when I see him."

"And you can fill him in with the video evidence of every fascinating moment of this ride," Gaby said with a smirk. "Better hope your battery doesn't run out and leave him hanging."

"Don't worry, I made sure I was fully charged before we set out," Becky told her. Not too long ago, Gaby's snarky comment might have made her bristle, but now they were such good friends, it was a welcomed joke. "Anyway, the filming isn't only for Alex. My followers like to keep up on the latest happenings, whatever they may be."

Heather giggled. "How many followers are you up to now? Is it six, or seven?"

"Eight," Becky said proudly. "That's more than ever before! Horse-some, right?"

Zoe laughed. Becky's vlog covered a range of subjects: Bob, the stables, Bob, her friends, Bob, interesting snacks, and still more Bob. It might have only a few followers, but those followers were loyal. Becky had found lots of interesting material to add to the vlog, between the quest to help the wild herd, the team tryouts, the mayor's advertising campaign to bring more visitors to the island, and more.

Zoe nudged Raven gently with her left leg to turn him onto the next road.

"It's way hard to believe we're spending so much time cleaning up the east wing of Pin's castle," Aaron said with a snort. "Shouldn't a duke have servants to do that stuff?"

Zoe just smiled again. It had been over a year, but sometimes she still had trouble believing that her boyfriend was a real, live duke. To her, he was just Pin, the kindest, most sensitive, horse-lovingest, sometimes prickly and confounding boy she'd ever met. Pin had spent part of his recently inherited fortune buying Bright Field Stables and rebuilding it after a fire. Then he'd spent more remodeling an unused part of the stables into a top-notch equine medical facility. Now he was finally turning his attention to the family castle, which Arthur had cleaned, but the east wing was still a little messy.

"Pin would never hire servants full stop," Winnie reminded Aaron. "He'd rather spend money on his brand-new horse hospital."

"Horsepital," Becky corrected her. "Speaking of which, I should take some more footage of the horses for the vlog soon. Scout is getting so big!"

Zoe glanced back again at Becky, who had stopped to film a patch of wildflowers beside the road. "Your followers are nature lovers, huh?" she commented.

"What? No," Becky said. "I mean yes, I suppose some of them are. But I'm also filming anything cool or interesting that I see. Heather said her mum might do another ad about the island soon, and who knows? Maybe she'll use some of my footage."

"Cool!" Aaron looked impressed. "That could be your ticket to Hollywood, baby."

Zoe laughed. "Or maybe not. But a new ad is a good

idea." She glanced at Heather. "Maybe now that her own daughter is riding at Bright Fields, she'll actually include us!" The mayor's previous ads trying to entice more visitors to the island had featured many good things about the island, but the list of attractions hadn't included the stables.

"Awesome idea, Zoe!" Winnie exclaimed. She glanced at Becky. "I mean, horse-some idea! Becky, you should totally make your own ad to show the mayor—I bet she'd use it. I would love to be able to prove myself like that."

"Yeah, do it!" Aaron urged. "I can help. I grew up in LA—I know a ton about showbiz. Plus, I've made a video before."

Gaby looked amused. How could she have forgotten Aaron's video? It was fantastic. "Right. I'm sure the mayor's really going to hire a bunch of kids as her ad agency."

Becky turned to Heather. "You'll convince your mum to look at my footage, though, right?"

"Sure, I can ask her." Heather squinted at the shady road ahead. "Hey, I think there's a shortcut to the castle grounds through there," she added, pointing. "Let's take it."

"What?" Becky exclaimed, actually lowering her phone camera for a moment. "Uh-uh, no way, forget it, we totally can't! That's Twisted Beech Wood. Everyone says it's haunted!"

Jade laughed. "Then I'd think you'd want to cut through there even more," she teased. "You're the one who was so keen on tracking down Ghost Pony, remember?"

Zoe remembered. That had been one of their first adventures together—one that had helped turn the three of them into Pony Squad. Now the Pony Squad included Gaby, too. "Yeah, maybe you'll catch a ghost on film, Becky," she said with a smile. "That'd impress your followers for sure!"

Becky rolled her eyes. "Don't be silly, ghosts don't show up on film." She pursed her lips. "Or wait—is that vampires?"

"Never mind." Gaby was already turning her horse toward the trail Heather had pointed out. "I'm down for a shortcut."

"Wait, no!" Winnie cried. "Becky, are there really ghosts in there? We shouldn't go if it might be dangerous."

Gaby shot a wicked smile over one shoulder. "Even better—I'm always up for a little danger, too. I'm going this way. Follow me if you dare!"

Gaby was riding Jet, a horse she loaned from Holloway. She softly nudged Jet, sending him scrambling up a bank and into the shade of the forest. Zoe rolled her eyes. That was so Gaby! She liked to play it tough, and maybe she was—growing up in foster care did that to you. But Zoe had seen her softer side, especially since the two of them had been sharing a room at Zoe's grandfather's house near the stables.

"Don't worry, Winnie," Zoe said, turning her horse toward the shortcut. "Raven and I will protect you from any ghosts. Anyway, Gaby and Heather are right—this should definitely get us to the castle faster."

When she glanced back, Winnie still looked worried. "Raven is the only horse that could probably protect us from ghosts," she said. It looked like she was lost in thought for a moment. Then she asked, "Are you guys sure this is a good idea?"

"Why not?" Aaron said with a grin. "Let's go, pardners—giddyup!"

With a cowboy-style whoop, he rode into the woods after Gaby. "Come on, Win, it'll be fine," Heather said. "There's no such thing as ghosts, anyway."

"She's right," Becky told Winnie. "I was just kidding around. There isn't a ghost in there. Probably not, anyway. And if there are, don't worry, Bob and I are experienced ghost hunters." She turned the camera toward herself. "Ghost log, day one—entering Twisted Beech Wood . . ." Then she rode on up the bank after the others.

With a shrug, Jade did the same. "O-okay," Winnie said, her voice quavering only slightly. "If Becky says it's safe, then I'm not worried at all. At least not very much."

"That's the spirit." Zoe grinned. "Pun totally intended!"

Soon all seven riders were winding their way through the wood, past gnarled, ancient trees whose branches blocked most of the sun's rays and turned the ground into a dappled tapestry of fallen leaves and brush. Zoe looked around with interest. Even after more than a year on the island, she was always amazed by the interesting and beautiful new places that seemed to lie around every bend.

Would Zoe ever know all the island's secrets?

"This is cool," she said. "I mean, it's only like a five-minute ride from the castle, but I've never—hey, Raven, stop!"

She'd let the reins go slack as they walked after Gaby's horse. Now she quickly gathered them up, trying to control Raven, who was suddenly spinning and lifting his forelegs in a semi-rear.

"Help!" Winnie cried at the same time as the sweet, quiet school pony she was riding took a quick step sideways. "Casper is spooking!"

"What was that?" Becky turned and pointed her camera to one side. "Did you see it? I told you there are ghosts in here!"

Zoe glanced that way just in time to see a flash of something white disappear into a thick gorse bush. "Raven, stop!" she cried. "Seriously!"

She finally got the big, black horse to settle down, though he continued to snort and prick his ears at every tiny sound. Meanwhile, Jade leaned down and grabbed Casper's bridle.

"It's okay, Winnie," she said. "Casper just got startled and jumped a bit, but he's fine now, see?"

"O-okay." Winnie looked pale, but she took a deep breath. "Was it really a ghost?"

"Doubtful," Zoe said. "Probably a bird or something."

"It might've been a ghost, though," Becky argued. "This area of the forest is supposed to be super haunted, remember? And the horses spooked at it!"

"Not most of them," Gaby said. "Jet didn't turn a hair. And everyone knows Raven is way too sensitive."

"Hey!" Zoe protested. She looked around at the rest of the group. As Gaby had said, Jet seemed unconcerned about the commotion. Jade's mount, Major, had his ears pricked at the gorse bush but was standing still. The other two ponies, Princess and Paolo, were also behaving themselves. Bob was taking advantage of the situation by nibbling on some leaves.

Jade laughed. "She's right; Raven has spooked at some pretty weird things, Zoe."

"Yeah. And maybe Casper was just jumping out of the way so Raven didn't run him over," Aaron said with a grin.

Becky pulled Bob away from the tasty leaves and rode closer to the gorse bush, filming it all the way. "I still think it was a ghost," she said. "I might need to come back here later and—hey! Bob, quit eating the bush; I'm trying to film it!"

Winnie patted Casper. The pony had long since recovered from his minor spook and now looked sleepy. But his rider still looked uncertain. "Do you really think it could be a real ghost, Becky?" Winnie asked.

"Never say never!" Becky peered through the viewfinder, scanning the area.

"Whatever." Gaby urged her horse forward. "You guys can play ghost police later, okay? Let's go already."

$\mathcal{F}$rom the outside, the east wing of the duke's castle looked solid, silent, and impassive, the secrets of generations of island royalty hidden behind its ancient stone walls. But when Zoe and her friends entered, they found that today at least, the inside was bustling with activity. A stout, cheerful-looking older woman with rosy cheeks and a mass of bright red curls piled atop her head was standing in the middle of the great hall, calling out instructions to a crew of half a dozen young men and women wielding brooms, dust pans, and mops.

"Wow," Zoe said as she stepped in and looked around. "Maybe Pin doesn't need our help after all!"

"On the contrary, miss." Pin's elderly butler, Arthur, bowed slightly as he closed the heavy door behind Zoe's group. "I'm afraid the old pile needs all the help it can get."

Pin had been over near the window talking to one of the workers. When he spotted the new arrivals, he hurried over, shooting Zoe a special smile. "Thanks for coming, guys," he said with a slight grimace. "Arthur's right. This place is a mess. I had never even stepped into the east wing before. I'm starting to think I should just lock the doors and walk away."

"Don't despair, your grace." Arthur nodded toward the red-haired woman. "Miss Imogen will help put it right."

"Who's Miss Imogen?" Zoe shot a curious look at the woman, who immediately turned and waved at the group.

"Hello, hello," she sang out, hurrying over. "None of this 'Miss' business, all right? It's just Imogen. Arthur here should know better than to mess about with formalities—why, the two of us have known each other since we were wee things in nappies!" She laughed heartily.

"Imogen runs a cleaning business on the mainland," Pin told Zoe and the others. "Arthur convinced her to come over for a week or so to help give the east wing a serious deep cleaning."

"That's right. Had to offer my best workers a few creative bribes to make the trip over." Imogen leaned closer and winked. "For instance, Nigel there just loves stinky French cheeses, so I promised him—ay, Nigel! Careful of that mirror!" She suddenly rushed off toward one of the young men working at the far side of the room.

"So that's Imogen, huh?" Zoe smiled at Pin. "She seems . . . energetic."

"We'll all have to be, if we expect to get this place tidied this century." Jade looked around worriedly.

"Too right," Gaby muttered.

Heather giggled. "My mum still can't believe I volunteered to clean up somebody else's rooms, since she says I never clean mine."

Becky smiled. "We're ready, Pin. Where do you want us to start?"

For the next hour or more, Zoe and her friends threw themselves into the task at hand. They scrubbed floors, swept dusty cobwebs out of corners, polished ancient woodwork, shifted heavy old furniture, and more. Bit by bit, the great room started to look less like the setting of a horror movie and more like a grand duke's castle—or the east wing of it, anyway.

Finally, Zoe stopped to rest and realized she hadn't checked on Raven or the other horses in a while. She found a window facing the lawn where they'd left them to graze, but the old panes were too grubby to see through.

"Excuse me," she said to a young woman who was scrubbing at some soot marks on a fireplace nearby. "Can I borrow that sponge for a sec? I need to clear a view to check on our horses."

"Of course. Here, I'll do it." The young woman hurried over and wiped a spot clean.

"Thanks. I'm Zoe, by the way," Zoe said with a smile.

"Hi, Zoe. I'm Bea," the young woman said, smiling back. "Did you say 'horses'? Oh, I wish my daughter Trixie was here—she's such an animal lover!"

Zoe remembered what Imogen had said about having to convince the workers to accompany her to the island. "Is your daughter still on the mainland?" she asked Bea. "You must miss her."

The young woman pushed back a strand of blond hair. "Oh, no, she came along with me," she said. "I told Imogen I couldn't leave her for an entire week. She understood, and found us a sweet little cottage near here to stay in." She laughed. "And that's not all, she even—"

"Zoe, Jade, guys, come quick!" Becky shouted at that moment.

"Oops." Zoe quickly glanced out at the horses, who looked fine. "Sorry, I'd better see what that's about. Thanks again!"

She rushed over to Becky, who was kneeling over a

dusty, old wooden crate. Judging by the skid marks on the wooden floorboards, Zoe guessed that her friend had just dragged the box out from beneath a table.

Jade slid to a stop at the same moment. "What's wrong?" she asked breathlessly.

Becky looked up at them, beaming. "Check out this box of cool old books I just found! Especially this one—*Legacy of the Dukes: Tales of the Unexplained*. Totally horse-some, right?"

Zoe traded an amused glance with Jade. Becky loved exploring the myths and legends of the island—the weirder and spookier, the better. For instance, the previous Valentine's Day weekend the whole group had tracked down the mythical Maid's Stone, which they'd learned about from an old map and other materials found in the castle.

Pin had heard Becky's shout, too. He joined them. "What's going on?" he asked.

"Becky found some dusty old books about your family's ghost stories or something," Zoe told him with a smile. "Watch out, or she'll steal them and enlist Ghost Pony to help her solve all the mysteries!"

Pin smiled back. "It's all right, Becky. You can keep whichever books you like. It's the least I can do after asking you guys to work so hard."

"Oh my Bob, really? Thanks, Pin!" Becky hugged *Legacy of the Dukes* to her chest. "I can't wait to read it!"

Jade plucked it away from her. "Might want to clean it first, Becky," she said, nodding at her friend's shirt, which now had a book-shaped dirt mark on it.

Becky swiped at the mark. "Oops."

Jade leaned down to examine the other books in the crate. "These all look like local titles," she commented. "There's even one about the old hotel—the one that used to be on the site of Mia's dad's new place."

"Interesting." Pin glanced at the book. "But I suppose it's not really Mia's dad's place anymore, is it? It's that Geoff guy's now."

Becky nodded and shivered. "Let's just hope he doesn't scare away all the guests!"

Zoe laughed. Geoff was a local man whose family had been in the hotel business for generations. He'd taken over the brand-new Firefly Hotel when Mia's father had been busted. "Yeah, Geoff looks a little scary," she agreed. "That's probably why the mayor hired him as her bodyguard before. But he seems to know what he's doing when it comes to running a resort, so I guess that's the important thing."

There was a clatter of rushed footsteps nearby. Zoe looked over to see Heather and Winnie emerging from the next room. Both of the younger girls looked freaked out. Gaby was behind them, though she appeared more amused than alarmed. "Oh my gosh, it's so gross!" Heather exclaimed. "Winnie just picked up this little wooden table thingy . . ."

"And there's a huge spider's nest under it!" Winnie's eyes were wide. "Seriously, there must be a billion baby spiders there!"

"Probably more like a trillion," Gaby said in a light-hearted way. Then she locked eyes with Zoe. "Why don't you go in there and take care of it, Zoe?"

"Me? Why me?" Zoe protested. She wasn't afraid of spiders, exactly. But she didn't relish the thought of dealing with a trillion of them, either!

Bea was scrubbing a baseboard nearby. She looked up with a smile. "I can do it," she said, reaching for a broom. "I don't mind."

"No, I think Zoe really wants to do it." Gaby smirked.

Zoe crossed her arms over her chest. "Says who? I think you're just trying to get me to do it so *you* don't have to do it. Scared of spiders, Gaby?"

"Hardly." Gaby rolled her eyes. "But I think we all would much prefer them out of the castle. *Pin* would, anyway. So, how about this? If you're not afraid, get in there and re-home those spiders. I'm sure they'd like it outside more than inside, anyway. I *dare* you."

Becky looked up from the old book, which she'd been paging through. "Ooh, a dare!" she exclaimed.

Zoe frowned. She never backed down from a dare—and she wasn't about to start with a silly one like this! "Oh yeah?" she said, stepping toward the doorway. "Fine, I'll re-home those spiders. All trillion of them, okay? But, Gaby, I dare *you* to help me do it."

"What? You can't dare me to help you with something I already dared you to do!" Gaby said. "That doesn't even make sense."

By then Aaron had wandered over to see what was going on. "Ooh! Sounds like Gaby's afraid of spiders!" he jeered. "Look out, Gaby, there's one crawling around on your head right now!"

"There is? Where?" Winnie quickly jumped away from Gaby, peering toward the older girl's head nervously.

Aaron was grinning broadly, his gaze jumping from Zoe to Gaby and back again as if watching a tennis match. "I think you're both afraid, but you won't admit it," he said.

"What?" Becky, Jade, and Heather chorused, turning to glare at him.

He raised his hands in surrender. "I just call 'em like I see 'em."

Zoe snorted. "Ignore him. I'm more interested in

hearing whether Gaby is too chicken to go in there with me and re-home those spiders. What do you say, Gaby? The dare stands."

Gaby just rolled her eyes. "Whatever," she said. "I still say it's not a real dare. But either way, it's no big deal. Let's do this."

Gaby and Zoe each squared their shoulders. They quietly headed to the door, dreading the hour-long or so dare that re-homing the spiders would be. Then they pulled the door open . . .

Zoe breathed a sign of relief. There were no spiders there after all.

"All that hubbub for nothing," Gaby said, though Zoe could tell she was pleased, too.

But Zoe knew her cousin Aaron better than anybody. She motioned Gaby to come closer.

"On the count of three, let's scream together," Zoe said. Gaby might not have known Zoe's plan, but since they were friends, it didn't really matter. "One . . . two . . . *three*!"

"Aaaah!" the girls cried out in unison.

"Aah!" came a louder, more shriek-worthy voice from inside.

Zoe smiled.

"Got him," she said, and she and Gaby high-fived.

3

*Z*oe smiled as she watched the horses in the paddock on the other side of the fence. "Scout is growing so fast, isn't he?" she commented as the playful colt let out a buck with his gangly legs. She, Gaby, Jade, and Becky had come to check on the horses.

Gaby never took her eyes off the horses as she leaned on the paddock fence. "He's great," she said.

"Hey, listen to this, guys!" Becky called out. She was sitting cross-legged on the ground nearby, paging through the book she'd taken from the castle. "Remember Peter the Young? The sad-looking kid duke from the old portraits?"

Zoe nodded. There were large oil portraits of all the past dukes hanging in the castle corridors—Peter the Wise, Peter the Mad, and many more. The portrait of Peter the Young stood out, since he was the only child of the bunch.

"I remember," Jade said.

"His whole story's in here. He had a puppy who was always running away, and one day Peter was chasing him, and, well, things didn't turn out so well for him."

"That's awful," Zoe said.

Becky was still reading. "Ooh, I know the spot they're describing here," she said. "It's that tall cliff overlooking the moon-shaped cove near the lilac grove—we ride past there all the time!"

"Moonlight Cliff," Jade said. "I know exactly where you mean. It's sad to think of something so horrible happening in such a gorgeous spot."

Zoe nodded, recognizing the place they meant.

"Ooh! And this is interesting," Becky said, still scanning the page. "It says here that the hound appeared as a ghost after the accident!"

Gaby turned away from watching the horses with a skeptical look on her face. "A ghost dog? Really?"

"Uh-huh." Becky bent closer over the book, her voice taking on a ghostly tone. "Apparently, the dog can be heard barking at night. If you listen really closely, that is!"

"Wow." Zoe wandered over and glanced down at Becky's book. "Good thing the ghost dog hasn't appeared lately, then. I wouldn't want it messing with any of us."

"Or has it?" Becky glanced up at her. "It says here that one of the common spots to hear the ghost dog barking is . . . Twisted Beech Wood!"

"Cue dramatic music," Gaby said with a snort. "Come on, Becky. You don't really believe this stuff, do you?"

"Oh, but she does," Jade said with a smile.

Becky didn't respond, instead turning the next page. "Hmm, that's all it says about the ghost dog, except that he's also been seen haunting the top of the cliff where the accident happened," she said. "Oh! But the next chapter sounds like a good one. It's called 'The Lost Treasure of Peter the Young.'"

"He had *treasure*, too?" Zoe said. "Too bad that name's taken. We might have to call Pin 'Peter the Old.'"

Zoe laughed. Pin's real name was Peter, just like his ancestors. "Just don't try to call him that," she added. "You know he hates being called 'Peter,' let alone 'duke' or 'sir' or anything fancy. And don't even joke about painting his portrait to hang in the corridor—I did once, and he refused to speak to me for like a week!"

Jade and Gaby laughed. But Becky was reading and didn't seem to hear. "Listen to this!" she blurted out suddenly, jabbing one finger at the page. "It says here that the treasure was never found!"

"What treasure is that, Becky?" Zoe asked, still smiling at the thought of Pin scowling out from a formal portrait.

"Peter the Young's! Aren't you listening?" Becky exclaimed.

"We heard that part," Jade told her. "But what sort of treasure? A chest of old valuable coins?"

"My guess is a jewel-encrusted space heater, to warm up that old castle," Zoe joked. "That's what I'd treasure if I lived there, anyway."

Becky turned the page forward, then back again. She frowned slightly. "Actually, it doesn't say exactly what the treasure is," she said. "Just that he buried his most valued possession on the moors."

"On the moors? That's not very specific—this island has more than its fair share of moors," Zoe said.

"No, there's more," Becky said. "It says 'he buried them in full view of moonlight, where he could hear the voice of the sea 'neath the shadow of the island's heart.' Hmm. I wonder what that means?"

"Beats me," Gaby said with a shrug. "And I'm not sure it's worth trying to figure it out if you don't even know what the treasure is."

"Or whether it's still there," Zoe added.

Becky rolled her eyes. "Of course it's still there! The book says it's never been found."

"Right. The book"—Jade plucked the volume out of her hands, then flipped to the front—"that was published, oh, sixty-five or so years ago? That book?"

Becky grabbed it back. "It's probably still there," she said. "At least it's worth having a look, right?" She turned back to the chapter about the treasure. Then she gasped. "Hey, I think I just figured out what the treasure is!"

She held up the book, which showed a portrait of Peter the Young. Zoe squinted at it.

"That's a different portrait than the one at the castle," Jade commented.

Becky nodded eagerly. "Check it out—see that super-fancy and valuable-looking jeweled medallion brooch he's wearing? And the way he's touching it, almost as if . . ."

"As if it's his most valued possession," Zoe said, guessing what Becky was thinking. "You could be right, though."

"Of course I'm right!" Becky bounced up and down with excitement. "If we find that treasure, Pin could use the money to run the horsepital!"

"I'm sure he'd like that," Gaby said.

"Exactly! Or he could display the treasure at the castle with all the other old stuff from his ancestors." Becky jumped to her feet. "I mean, the place is practically a museum, anyhow—maybe he could actually get people to pay to come see it!"

Zoe traded a knowing look with Jade. Becky and her little brother had to pay all of Bob's expenses themselves, which meant Becky was always in search of a money-making scheme.

Becky took a few steps toward the stable yard. Then she paused and looked back at the others, who hadn't moved. "Well? What are you waiting for?" she demanded. "Come on, let's get our horses tacked up again and go search for that treasure!"

"No, thanks," Gaby said. "It's nearly dinnertime."

"Right," Zoe said. "*Bob's* dinnertime. Do you really think he's going to want to ride out onto the moors right now?"

Becky stopped, momentarily looking uncertain. Then she shrugged. "We won't be long," she said. "We can just scope out the nearest moors to see if there are any heart-shaped rocks or something like that out there."

She raced off again, disappearing down the alley leading into the courtyard. Jade sighed. "I think she's serious. Come on, let's see if we can talk some sense into her before Bob dumps her in a gully and runs back to the stables without her."

Zoe laughed. "Let's go."

She took off down the alley with Jade at her heels. As they rounded the corner toward Bob's stall, Zoe skidded to a stop just in time to avoid crashing into Becky, who was standing still, staring across the yard.

"Oof!" Jade blurted out as she bumped into Zoe. "Hey, Becky, what are you doing?"

Becky didn't answer. Zoe followed her gaze and saw two people in front of a stall across the way. They were huddled with their heads very close together, talking in low voices that didn't carry to where Zoe and the others were standing.

"What's going on?" Gaby asked, coming up behind them. "Is that Alex and Susie?"

Just then Susie looked up and saw them. She stepped back quickly from Alex, shot the girls a half smile, then rushed off and disappeared into her horse's stall.

Meanwhile, Alex loped across the yard to join Becky and the others. "There you are!" he said cheerfully, giving Becky's arm a squeeze and the other girls a warm smile. "How was the castle-cleaning mission?" He glanced at the book clutched in Becky's hand. "Hey, what's that?"

"This?" Becky glanced at the book, blinked, then smiled. "Oh! Wait until you see it—it's horse-some! I found it at the castle, and Pin said I could keep it, and . . ."

With that, she was off and running, telling Alex all about the book and the legend of Peter the Young's hidden treasure, and his dog that howled for three days.

"That was odd, eh?" Gaby murmured in Zoe's ear. "Alex and Susie looking all cozy like that . . ."

Zoe glanced back at her with a frown. "What do you mean? They were just talking."

Gaby raised her eyebrows. "If you say so."

Becky was leading the way toward Bob's stall as she chatted with Alex. As they reached it, the door swung open. The handsome young head trainer and stable manager emerged holding an empty bucket. Becky and Jade had nicknamed him "Hot Marcus" long ago, but now he was dating Mia. That didn't stop them from using the nickname, though!

"There you are," Marcus said, looking at Gaby. "I was about to text you. It's time to mix the evening feed, and I was hoping not to have to do it by myself."

Gaby nodded. She worked at the stables to cover her expenses. "On it," she said. "Sorry, Becky. Guess you'll have to go treasure hunting another time."

"Treasure hunting?" Marcus cocked an eyebrow and smiled. "Uh-oh. What are you up to this time, Becky?"

Before she could respond, the Breakfast Club came running toward them. "Becky, there's a really cool lizard out by the manure pile," Winnie exclaimed.

"Yeah, we thought you could film it for the mayor's new commercial!" Aaron added excitedly.

"Sorry, gang," Becky told them. "I might have to take a little break from that project. I have something much more important to do." Suddenly, she stood up straighter. "Oh! But maybe when I find the treasure, Pin will let me use part of the proceeds to increase my film budget. That way I'd be sure to catch the mayor's eye!"

"What treasure?" Heather asked, looking confused.

"Becky thinks one of Pin's ancestors hid this valuable old brooch full of jewels and stuff out on the moors," Zoe told them.

"I don't think so—I know so!" Becky held up the book. "It's all right in here."

"Cool!" Aaron said. "So if you find this thing, what kind of film budget are we talking about?"

Becky shrugged. "The brooch looks super swanky, so I suppose the sky's the limit."

Aaron rubbed his hands together. "Great! That means we could spring for some super-dope special effects, maybe hire a Hollywood A-lister to do a voice-over . . ."

"Let's not go crazy here," Jade said. "We don't even know the treasure is still out there."

"And we don't know it's not," Becky retorted. "So

instead of wasting time talking about it, let's hurry up and decide whether there's time to ride out looking before dinnertime."

Marcus had ducked into the next stall to retrieve another bucket, but now he popped out. "I vote no, for what it's worth," he said. "You know Bob—his stomach has a timer on it."

Becky looked unconvinced. "Okay, but there's time for a short ride—you haven't even mixed the feed yet! What do you say, Alex? You'll come with me, right?"

She looked at her boyfriend. So did Zoe—just in time to catch Alex checking his watch. He looked up with a sheepish smile. "Rain check, okay? I promised I'd be home early today. I probably should get going right now, actually."

"But I didn't even finish telling you about the treasure," Becky protested.

"Text me later, okay?" Alex bent to give Becky a peck on the cheek, then hurried off.

"Wow, he seemed to be in a big hurry," Gaby said loudly. "Wonder what that was about?"

Zoe shot her an annoyed look. Why was she acting like there was something suspicious about Alex all of a sudden? Was it just because they'd seen him talking to Susie? That seemed like a stretch even for Gaby, who seemed to be wary of everyone and everything.

Fortunately, Becky didn't seem to have noticed. She and Aaron were back to talking about special effects and other plans.

"I won't have much time to do the actual filming myself, though," Becky told the Breakfast Club. "Well, aside from filming the actual treasure hunting, of course. But you guys might have to take over the rest of it for a while. You know—until I find the loot."

"On it!" Aaron said immediately. "I can handle the camerawork—I've done it before, if you remember. And I'm good at it, right, Zoe? Tell them!"

"Yeah, he's good with a camera," Zoe confirmed with a smile. "The whole family says so."

Heather shrugged. "Fine. You can be the cameraman," she told Aaron. "But I know what kind of stuff my mum is probably looking for; plus, I know lots about PR from her—that's public relations, in case you don't know."

"I knew that," Aaron retorted quickly. "I mean, I've heard of it . . ."

"What can I do?" Winnie sounded a bit forlorn. "I don't really know anything much about making movies, or public relations."

"You can be in charge," Becky told her. "After all, you're my mini-me, right?" She tugged on one of the younger girl's blond braids, which matched her own. "You tell the others what to do."

"What?" Heather exclaimed.

"Hey, no way!" Aaron said at the same time.

Just then Bob stuck his head out over his half door. He gave Becky a shove with his nose and let out a nicker.

"Oops. That's Bob's 'where's my dinner?' call," Becky said. She sighed. "Guess that means I'll have to wait until tomorrow to start searching for the treasure."

"You mean day after tomorrow," Jade corrected her. "You told me you're going with your mum and dad to visit your gran tomorrow, remember?"

"Oh, right!" Becky smacked herself on the forehead. "Talk about bad timing! I hope someone else doesn't find the treasure while I'm stuck drinking tea and talking about rosebushes."

Zoe smiled. "I don't think you have to worry about that," she said, turning to head toward the feed room to help Marcus. "If it's still there after all these years, it'll wait another day."

"All warmed up, ladies?" Marcus strode into the riding arena. "Good. Let's get started."

Zoe and Gaby were already in the arena on their horses. Zoe halted Raven in front of Marcus and looked down at him. "Don't act like *we* were the ones keeping *you* waiting," she said. "We've been out here warming up for ages."

"Right." Gaby stopped Jet beside Raven. "Although, I suppose you can't put a time limit on helping Mia wrap Firefly's legs, hmm? Even though she seems perfectly capable of doing that sort of thing on her own."

Zoe watched Marcus carefully. He and Mia used to date and now they were back together. They'd been friends for a long time, and had been through a lot. Zoe was glad to see Marcus so happy.

Zoe turned Raven and sent him along the rail at a walk. "Let's get this lesson started. What's first, boss?"

Marcus stepped to the center of the arena, tapping the riding crop he was holding against the top of his tall boot. "Let's start with some easy dressage moves—leg yield along the rail, please."

Raven and Jet had just finished their leg yields when the Breakfast Club hurried into view from the direction of the courtyard. Aaron was in the lead, carrying a small digital video camera. Winnie was right behind him with a clipboard, while Heather was tapping away on her phone.

"Oh, good, there's finally someone riding out here," Heather said. "Can we film you guys?"

"We want to get tons of horse footage for the ad," Winnie put in.

"Fine with me if Zoe and Gaby don't mind," Marcus said.

"I don't mind," Zoe said, while Gaby just shrugged.

"Cool!" Aaron lifted his camera, aiming it toward Raven. "We need more action shots. Then I can use slo mo to make some of them look really awesome . . ."

"Look, you can watch and film or whatever," Marcus said. "But stay out of the way—and keep quiet, all right?"

The younger kids all nodded. Zoe turned Raven at the end of the arena. "What's next, Marcus?" she called out.

"How about some jumping?" Heather suggested. "That would look good in the ad."

Marcus shot her a look. "What did I just say about keeping quiet?"

"I'm just saying, it would be nice if you did some jumping now," Heather said. "The bigger the better!"

Zoe grinned. Heather wasn't very good at keeping quiet. Then again, she probably got that from her mother, the mayor, who loved nothing more than giving speeches and talking to people.

"Quiet," Marcus ordered once more. Then he turned back to the riders. "Let's continue with our flatwork—I really want the horses listening to your aids, all right?"

For the next few minutes, Marcus put the two horses through a series of basic exercises on the flat. Raven was younger than Jet and hadn't been in training as long. But he had come a long way since the early days, when he'd been so wild that Zoe had trouble trotting him in a circle without problems. These days, it felt as if Raven could do anything!

When Marcus called for a halt, Zoe patted her horse proudly. "Good boy. Since you did that so well, maybe Marcus will reward us by finally letting us do some jumping, hmm?"

Marcus smiled and glanced toward a line of jumps set

up in the center of the arena. "You read my mind."

"Awesome!" Zoe said. "Looks like a gymnastic—fun!"

"Finally, something interesting," Aaron said, raising his camera again.

Marcus ignored him, focusing on Zoe and Gaby. "Fun and educational, for you and your horses," he said, stepping over to raise the top pole on one of the jumps. "You'll start by trotting the horses through the poles on the ground, nice and steady. That should set them up perfectly for the crossrail. They should land at canter, and it's two strides to the vertical, then another two to the final jump."

"Got it." Gaby gathered her reins and gave Jet a careful nudge with her heel to turn him toward the line of jumps. "We'll go first."

"Why does she get to go first?" Zoe complained.

Gaby stuck out her tongue as she rode past. "Because I called it," she said.

Zoe rolled her eyes. Marcus laughed. "Don't fret, Zoe," he said. "Use this—watch her go through, and plan your trip accordingly."

"Fine." Zoe slumped in her saddle, pretending to pout.

But she sat up when Gaby turned Jet to begin the line. The elegant black horse picked up a brisk trot, lifting each foot carefully as he stepped over the poles. He surged forward after that, almost breaking into a canter before the crossrail. Gaby managed to keep him at trot, but Jet overjumped the crossrail and had trouble fitting two strides in before the next jump. But Gaby didn't lose her cool—she collected him on landing, and the final jump went much better.

"Nice recovery," Marcus called to her. "But you'll need to be ready for that trot jump next time. Jet is—"

He cut himself off as a tinny ringtone blasted out from his pocket. Marcus pulled out his phone and glanced at it.

"Hey, no texting and riding," Zoe called to him. "Isn't that what you're always telling us?"

"Yes, but if you'll notice, I'm not riding." He shot her a smirk in return, then sighed. "Sorry, you two. The feed delivery's here, and nobody's around to sign the receipt. Won't take long. Can you entertain yourselves until I get back?"

"Of course we can," Gaby said.

"But we'll miss you!" Zoe added with a grin.

As soon as Marcus disappeared down the alley, Gaby glanced at Zoe. "Now what?" she said. "Should we keep on with the gymnastic or what?"

Zoe shrugged. "He'd probably want us to wait." Then

she glanced at the line of jumps and smiled. "Then again, I'm no mind reader. What do you say, Raven? Should we give it a try?"

"Do it!" Heather called from the rail. "Aaron, get ready."

"I was born ready!" Aaron lifted the camera as Zoe turned Raven toward the line of jumps.

"Easy, boy. We're just trotting now, okay?" Zoe murmured as they headed toward the poles. One, two, three, four—Raven trotted through them perfectly. He tossed his head, but stayed at a steady trot until he reached the first jump . . .

"Well done!" Gaby called out a moment later as Raven landed after the final jump. "That was foot perfect. Too bad Marcus didn't see it."

"Thanks." Zoe halted beside Jet, then gave Raven a pat. "What can I say? Jumping is kind of our thing."

"That was a little more interesting," Heather called, climbing up on the lower rail. "But still a little boring. Can you do something more exciting now?"

"Like what?" Gaby asked. "Light the jumps on fire and then jump them?"

Aaron's face lit up. "Yeah! That would be awesome!"

"Sorry, cuz," Zoe said with a laugh. "Not happening."

"The fire's probably not a good idea," Gaby agreed

with a wicked little smile. "But why not give the kiddos something fun? Like, um . . ." She paused, riding Jet in a little circle as she thought about it. Then her smile broadened. "Got it. You said jumping's your thing, right, Zoe? So let's make it a little more challenging. You could jump while singing karaoke!"

Zoe glanced at the jumps. "What, you mean sing a whole song while on my horse?"

"Yes, and ideally on key," Gaby said.

"Yes!" Aaron exclaimed. "Do it, Zoe!"

"I don't know." Winnie sounded uncertain. "That sounds kind of silly . . ."

"I'd be focusing entirely on the song," Zoe said, rolling her eyes.

But the Breakfast Club kids were still staring at them. "Well?" Heather called out. "Are you gonna do it, Zoe?"

"No way," Zoe called back.

"I don't blame you," Winnie said with a shiver. "I would never be able to sing in front of people, let alone whilst riding!"

"I guess Zoe doesn't *dare* do it, either," Gaby said. "Or do you?" She raised her eyebrows. "I mean, you never had to do that dare at the castle yesterday. So here's your chance to make up for it. I dare you, Zoe."

Zoe frowned.

"Don't be chicken," Gaby continued. "Are you going to do it or do I have to break it to everyone that Zoe Phillips backed down from a dare?" She glanced at the jumps before meeting Zoe's gaze again. "A pretty easy one, too."

Zoe glared back at her. Every time she thought she and Gaby were getting closer, starting to understand each other . . . she had to go and pull something like this!

"Shouldn't we be setting a good example for these younger riders?" Zoe waved a hand at the Breakfast Club. "I'm sure that's what Marcus would want us to do. Goofing off on the horses isn't exactly an example."

"Marcus isn't here." Gaby dropped her reins and crossed her arms, her challenging gaze never wavering. "The dare stands."

"Do it! Do it!" Aaron chanted.

"Come on, Zoe," Heather added. "It'll look really fun and cool in the video! A singing rider!"

Zoe sighed, shooting one last glare toward Gaby. "I guess," she said. "Hold still, Raven . . . quick, this is going to be interesting."

She dropped her reins on her horse's neck.

"All right, what song am I singing?" she said.

"Is that even a question?" Gaby laughed. "You're on

the island now, Miss America. You have to sing the British national anthem!"

Zoe nodded. Although she was American and had never learned the anthem in school, she heard her grandfather singing it around the house every now and then.

"Ready?" Gaby asked.

"As ready as I'll ever be," Zoe replied.

She gave Raven the signal it was time to go. And then Zoe began.

"God save our gracious Queen;
Long live our noble Queen:
God save the Queen."

A few members of the crowd started singing along. Zoe looked all around her. She had to admit it, it felt kind of fun to combine singing and horseback riding, all in one!

Zoe was about to finish on a high note and end the song when she heard a voice.

"Ahem!"

Zoe glanced over to see Marcus standing at the arena gate, arms crossed. How much had he seen?

"Oops," Zoe said, quickly lowering her arms. "Um, we were just . . ."

"Never mind." Marcus strode over to meet Raven as

the horse skidded to a halt nearby. "But at Bright Field Stables, we're *serious* about our horses here. In case you didn't know."

"Thanks, very helpful." Zoe glanced toward the Breakfast Club. All three of them were giggling, and Aaron shot her a thumbs-up. Oh well. Marcus was probably going to make her sing songs for the rest of the year after that stunt. But Zoe had to admit—it had been kind of fun!

That evening after dinner, Zoe was riding Raven at a walk along a quiet country lane when her phone pinged. She pulled it out—it was a text from Pin:

You still coming over?

Zoe smiled. "Looks who's impatient," she told Raven, who flicked an ear back briefly.

Zoe texted Pin back:

Be there in 5

Then she stuck her phone back in her pocket and looked around. "Actually, it'll probably be more like ten, unless we want to canter the rest of the way." She glanced down at her horse. "No, wait, I have a better idea. Let's try that shortcut again."

They were almost to the little trail through Twisted

Beech Wood. When they reached it, Zoe steered her horse up the bank. It was nearing dusk, making the wood seem spookier and more shadowy than ever. Raven was on alert as they picked their way along the winding trail.

"It's okay, boy," Zoe said. "Whatever Becky says, I'm sure there are no—"

She cut herself off with a gasp as a shrub shuddered nearby. A second later, something small and white dashed out of it, racing across the trail and disappearing into some other brush. Zoe wasn't sure in the dim light, but she thought it looked like . . . a dog?

But there wasn't much time to ponder that as Raven reared and then took off, racing through the wood with his head high and his breath coming in panicky snorts. "Raven, stop!" Zoe cried, trying to regain control. "It was just a dog—or something . . . Anyway, it was a lot smaller than you, so chill!"

But the horse ignored her, finally crashing out of the woods onto the castle grounds. A couple of people were walking along the path toward the wood, and jumped back at the horse's sudden appearance.

"Sorry, sorry!" Zoe called breathlessly, finally managing to bring Raven to a halt, though he kept prancing and snorting nervously. "We just, um . . . my horse spooked." Suddenly, she recognized the figures as two of the cleaners from Imogen's crew, including Bea, the young mother who'd helped her with the dirty window. "Oh, hello!"

"Hi, Zoe." Bea looked impressed as she stared at Raven. "Is that your horse? He's gorgeous!"

"Thanks." Zoe smiled, giving Raven a pat. "He's usually better behaved than this."

Just then she heard a whistle. Glancing forward, she saw Pin hurrying toward them. "There you are!" he said. Noticing the workers, he gave them a smile. "Thanks for the hard work today, guys."

The second cleaner tipped his hat to Pin. "Our pleasure, sir. Come on, Bea—I'll walk you home on my way."

Zoe waved to the pair as they continued on toward the wood. Then she smiled down at Pin. "Just so you know, Becky is totally going overboard with that old book you gave her. I know, I know, Becky going overboard—shocking, right? But she's ready to search the entire island for your old relatives' lost treasure. Oh, and she thinks a ghost dog is haunting the woods near here."

"A ghost dog?" Pin looked amused. "Sounds terrifying."

"I know, right?" Zoe grinned. "Apparently you can hear it bark. Worse yet, I think Raven and I just saw it! Becky's totally rubbing off on me."

Just then her phone pinged. Zoe pulled it out. "It's Becky. She wants to live video chat." Zoe was a little surprised. Normally Becky texted or posted to the Pony Squad group chat when she had something to say.

She slid down from the saddle and pulled the reins over Raven's head, allowing him to graze on the lawn nearby. Then she held up the phone so she and Pin could both see. When she clicked to accept the live chat, Becky's face filled the entire screen, looking excited.

"Guess what, Zoe?" Becky exclaimed. "Oh, hi, Pin. Guess what? We've gone viral!"

"Uh-oh," Pin joked. "Better call a doctor."

Becky blinked at him, then shook her head. "No, I'm serious," she said. "I know my followers don't like to be kept waiting for new material. So I posted the video that the Breakfast Club took earlier today—you know, the one of you and Gaby and Raven?"

Pin glanced at Zoe curiously. "What video?"

"Oh, it's great," Becky told him. "See, Gaby dares Zoe to sing a song while riding Raven, and Zoe totally rocks it! It's horse-some! And I'm not the only one who thinks so—people copied it to a bunch of other places—and now I have more than fifty followers!"

When Zoe arrived at Bright Fields the next morning, she was disappointed not to see Pin there. He'd promised to show up for a ride if he could, though he'd said he might not make it if the cleaners needed him to stay at the castle.

She pulled out her phone. Sure enough, there was a text from Pin saying he couldn't get away.

"Oh well," Zoe whispered, disappointed but not surprised. One of the many great things about Pin was that he always pitched in when there was work to do. That hadn't changed at all when he'd become a duke.

She looked around the stable yard. Pin might be missing, but it looked as if just about everyone else she knew was there. Jade was talking to Mia and Susie near the tack room. Marcus was examining his pony, Monty's, hoof, and Gaby was sweeping the courtyard. Alex was helping Becky groom Bob at the hitching rail. The Breakfast Club trio was filming it all.

"Zoe!" Becky looked up with a grin. "Great news. I'm up to sixty-one followers this morning!"

"Fab." Zoe headed toward Raven's stall. Her horse looked out and nickered when he saw her coming. "Hey, buddy," she greeted him, caressing his head. "What do you want to do today?"

Aaron heard her and looked over. "Don't make any plans, cuz," he called. "We have a great idea, and everyone needs to play."

"Play?" Alex said, looking up from fiddling with a knot in Bob's thick, multicolored mane. "What do you mean?"

Heather grinned. "That dare got loads of hits, right?" she said. "So let's give the people what they want!"

"Yes," Winnie added. "We can play a stables-wide game of Truth or Dare! Or Truth or *Mare*! You know, because of the horses."

"With cool dares and interesting truths," Heather continued.

Aaron held up his camera. "And film the whole thing for our adoring fans."

Zoe rolled her eyes. "Count me out."

"Me too," Mia said with a little frown. "Last time we played Truth or Dare it didn't go well, remember?"

Zoe grimaced as she realized what Mia was talking about. Previously, the gang had gathered on the beach for a picnic, and a game of Truth or Dare had broken out that had led to embarrassment and danger.

"Good point," Jade said. She looked at the Breakfast Club. "You three weren't here yet, but it was a bad scene."

"Never mind that." Becky dropped the brush she was using on Bob's shaggy legs and clapped her hands. "I think it's a great idea! I'm surprised I didn't think of it myself—must be too preoccupied with that treasure."

"Wait—" Zoe began.

"Maybe it's not the best idea," Winnie said at the same time. "What happens if we don't want to do a dare or tell a truth?"

"Well, you have to do a dare or tell the truth," Becky replied. "Us Bright Fields kids aren't scared of anything. Right?"

Aaron laughed. "Right!"

Zoe could see that Winnie looked uncomfortable, but before she could say anything else, Gaby dropped her broom and stepped forward.

"I'm game," she said. "Turn on the camera—I'll go first." She looked around with a mischievous smile as Marcus returned from taking the pony he'd been examining back to its stall. "Marcus. Truth or mare. I mean, dare?"

Marcus raised both hands. "Whoa, who said I was playing?"

"You scared?" Gaby taunted, stepping closer. "Think I'll ask you a question you don't want to answer truthfully?" Her eyes darted from him to Mia and back again, and her smile widened.

Marcus swallowed hard. "Er, fine. Dare, then. But nothing silly like singing a song in front of everyone, all right?"

"No rules," Gaby said. Then she shrugged. "But fine, we'll take it easy on your first time out." She looked around as if searching for inspiration. Her gaze settled on Becky, who as usual was dressed in clashing bright colors. "Got it. I dare you to show the world what color underpants you're wearing."

"Oh, snap!" Aaron shouted, while Heather, Becky, and Winnie shouted with laughter.

Alex grinned. "You gotta do it. She dared you!"

Marcus's cheeks flamed pink. He glanced around as if searching for an escape route.

"What's the big deal, Marcus?" Zoe asked, amused in spite of herself. "Everyone knows a proper guy like you has to be wearing tighty-whities, right? Big shocker there."

"Shows what you know," Marcus said, breaking into an embarrassed smile. "Fine, here goes . . ."

Turning his back to the others, he lowered his

breeches a few inches, revealing the top hem of his boxers, which were striped bright green and purple.

"Whoa, Marcus! That's not just horse-some, it's *coloriffic!*" Becky exclaimed.

"There, I did it." Marcus yanked his breeches back into place. Then he looked at Aaron, who was filming the whole thing. "But listen, you can't put that on the Internet."

"Says who?" Aaron hit a button on the camera and grinned. "Already uploaded."

"What?" Marcus exclaimed, his face going red again.

Mia laughed. "Don't be so uptight, Marcus," she said. "It's not a big deal."

Zoe shot her a surprised look. Mia was even more proper and stuffy than Marcus, never showing up anywhere without full makeup, perfect hair, and a carefully coordinated outfit. Then again, maybe she'd changed since her father had been revealed as a crook.

Marcus looked surprised by Mia's comment, too. But he smiled at her. "Whatever, I suppose you're right," he said. "Hang on. It's my turn to choose someone now, yeah?"

"Right," Gaby said quickly. "But you can't choose the same person who chose you." At Marcus's glare, she shrugged and leaned back against the hitching rail. "I don't make the rules."

"No, she's right," Becky said. "You have to choose someone different. Go on, Marcus."

"Okay," Marcus said. "Then, Becky, I suppose you're it. Truth or dare?"

"Truth!" Becky said. "Wait, no, dare! No, wait, maybe truth after all . . . hmm, I can't decide."

"Truth is boring," Aaron said. "Choose dare so we have something good to post."

"Yeah." Heather was looking at her phone. "Marcus's underpants aren't getting much interest so far. We need something better."

"Hey!" Marcus protested.

"No, they're right." Becky squared her shoulders. "Dare. Definitely dare."

"I know," Mia spoke up again. "Marcus, you should dare her to give Bob a proper groom. Haircut and all."

Becky glanced at Bob, who was dozing at the rail. Bob was lots of things, but being a fancy horse was not one of them.

Marcus chuckled. "Sorry, Mia," he said. "I wouldn't dare propose that dare. Bob wouldn't be Bob if he wasn't hairy."

"Right," Jade agreed. "He's like Samson—his hair is where his superpowers lie."

"Which superpowers would those be?" Mia demanded. "The power to eat everything in sight? Or perhaps the power to open stall doors and let himself out to cause trouble and poop on everything?"

Zoe traded an amused look with Jade. Okay, maybe Mia's father's troubles hadn't changed her *that* much . . .

"I love Bob, but let's be honest with ourselves. He's kind of a mess," Mia finished. Instantly, Zoe's gaze softened. After all, it was Bob who'd rescued Mia's favorite horse, Firefly, from a fire. Mia liked Bob, all things considered.

Marcus snapped his fingers. "I've got it," he announced. "Becky, I dare you to take Bob to the pier and convince at least three people to let him lick ice cream off their faces."

Becky blew out a breath, looking relieved. "Oh, is that all?" she said. "Easy-peasy. Bob loves ice cream. And people love Bob." She untied his lead rope from the hitching post. "Come on, everyone. Let's do this."

"Check it out." Winnie held out her phone. "Seventeen hits already!"

Zoe grinned as she watched the video. She'd already seen it all happen live, of course; most of the group had accompanied Becky and Bob on their dare, though Marcus had stayed behind to keep an eye on the stables, and Mia and Susie had opted to remain behind as well to groom their horses instead of making the long walk to the pier.

"I can't believe that grumpy old man said yes!" Heather exclaimed as the group huddled around to watch the video. They'd just arrived back at the yard, which was quiet and deserted aside from their group.

Zoe grinned as she watched Bob slobber all over the old man's face, licking off every last drop of ice cream.

"That guy used pistachio—it's one of Bob's favorites," Becky said.

"Shh. Here's where he licks the little kid and almost knocks him over," Gaby said.

Alex laughed. "That was hilarious!"

They watched the video all the way through. Then when Marcus, Mia, and Susie appeared, Aaron called them over to watch, too.

"Very nice," Mia said dryly, barely glancing at the screen. "Is this game over yet?"

"No way—It's my turn to choose." Becky grinned. "And I choose—you, Mia!"

"Oh, joy." Mia rolled her eyes. "Truth."

"What?" Becky's face fell. "No, don't choose truth! I have the perfect dare for you. You're going to love it."

Mia looked dubious. "Did I stutter? Truth, please."

"Oh, go on, Mia." Marcus elbowed her. "Don't break Becky's heart. Anyway, I did a dare, so don't be scared."

"I'm not scared." Mia crossed her arms and glanced at Marcus. Then she sighed. "Fine, whatever gets this over with faster. Dare, I suppose."

"Yay!" Winnie cheered. "Make sure it's something that'll look interesting on video, Becky."

"Don't worry, it will." Becky rubbed her hands together eagerly. "Mia, I dare you—to ride out with me to search for Peter the Young's brooch!"

Mia looked confused. "What?"

"Who's Peter the Young?" Susie asked.

"Pin's ancestor," Jade explained. "He had a dog who some people now think is a ghost. Meanwhile, Becky thinks his long-lost brooch is buried out on the moors."

Mia didn't look impressed. Zoe guessed that she was going to tell Becky she wasn't going to do it. "Don't worry, Becky," she said quickly. "If Mia backs out of the dare, I'll go with you."

"Me too," Jade said with a nod.

Mia glared at them. "Trying to make me look bad on video, are you?" She glanced at Aaron, who was filming away as usual. "I *don't* back out of dares. Even childish ones." She shifted her glare to Becky. "I suppose I'll get Firefly tacked up, then." She glanced at Susie. "Get Darcy ready. If I have to do this, you do, too."

"But it's not my dare," Susie protested. Seeing Mia's

expression, she shrugged. "But it's okay, I'll come."

"Good! I'll toss a saddle on Bob," Becky said.

"What do you say?" Zoe asked Jade. "Should we tag along, anyway?"

"No sense being left out of the fun," Jade said. "I'll go get Major."

"I'm coming, too," Gaby said. "I don't think there's any treasure out there, but if Becky's going to make Mia dig around on the moors I want to see it."

"Oh, you'll see it." Aaron held up his camera. "Everyone will see it."

Mia rolled her eyes. "Just hurry up and let's get this over with," she grumbled.

Becky grabbed Bob's saddle off the fence, then glanced at Alex. "Well? Better get your horse ready, too."

"Er . . ." Alex looked sheepish. "Actually, I'd better skip it," he said. "Atilla seemed a bit tired after our ride earlier. Plus, I have some stuff to do at home."

Susie stopped short halfway to the tack room. "Oops, I just remembered I'm supposed to go shopping with my mum today for back-to-school clothes. Sorry, guys, I'd better stay back, too."

"Oh." Becky looked disappointed. Then she shrugged and brightened. "All right, then. Come on, the rest of you— the Bright Fields Adventure Mission leaves in ten minutes!"

6

So where are we starting the hunt?" Zoe asked Becky. The group of brooch hunters—Zoe, Becky, Jade, Mia, Gaby, and the three Breakfast Club kids—was riding down the shady lane outside the stable yard.

"I've been thinking about that, actually," Becky said. She glanced over at Aaron, who was near the back of the group riding his usual pony, Paolo. "Make sure you have the sound turned up," she called to him. "I want everyone to hear everything."

"Got it, boss." Aaron shot her a quick thumbs-up with the hand not holding the camera, then returned it to Paolo's reins.

Becky nodded. "Okay. So I've been thinking about the line from the book about where Peter the Young buried the brooch . . ."

"'In full view of moonlight,'" Winnie quoted. "'Where he could hear the voice of the sea 'neath the shadow of the island's heart.'"

"Well, that's super helpful," Mia said sarcastically, steering Firefly around a hole in the road.

"Duh," Becky told her. "It's supposed to be mysterious. Otherwise the brooch would've been found ages ago!"

"Fair point," Gaby said, sounding amused.

"So do you have a theory, Becky?" Jade asked.

Becky nodded. "Remember how we rode through Twisted Beech Wood the other day?" she said. "Well, I noticed one of the crazy old trees in there has this branch that's shaped sort of like a heart. What if it's pointing us toward the right spot?"

"Makes as much sense as anything," Zoe said. "Let's go check it out."

They turned down the road to the castle with Zoe and Raven riding beside Becky and Bob at the head of the group. When they neared the turnoff for the shortcut, Raven let out a sudden snort and veered sideways.

"Hey," Becky said. "You almost bumped into us!"

"Sorry." Zoe tugged on one rein and carefully nudged Raven with her heel, trying to move him over. But the big black horse ignored her, staring into the wood with his head up and ears pricked.

"What's wrong?" Winnie called. "Is Raven looking for ghosts?"

Mia snorted. "Ghosts, really?" she said.

"Easy, Princess." Heather patted her pony, who was staring off into the wood now, too. "You don't need to look for ghosts. Raven's just being Raven."

"Hey, heads up!" Aaron called from the back of the line. "There's a car coming."

"Oh. Maybe that's why Raven's acting funny," Zoe said. "He probably heard it before we did."

The riders all moved their horses off to the side of the road across from the wood, where there was a wide verge. Then Zoe glanced back at the car, which was approaching slowly.

"Hey, it's one of the Firefly Hotel cars," Jade said.

Zoe nodded and shot a glance at Mia, wondering how it felt to be so suddenly reminded of her father's disgrace. But Mia didn't react, other than to lean forward and rub Firefly's neck. Zoe shrugged and turned her attention back to the car. When it came closer, she could see that Geoff was driving.

He slowed down even more as he passed the horses. "Morning, kids," he called with a wave. "Nice day for a ride."

"Sure is," Zoe called back, while the others waved or added hellos.

Geoff didn't stop, continuing a bit past the group and then resuming normal speed. Zoe was glad. He still seemed a bit scary!

She rode Raven back out into the road along with the others. A short distance farther along, Becky pointed.

"That's the tree I mean," she said. "See? It looks like a heart."

Jade tilted her head, looking uncertain. "I suppose if you squint a bit . . ."

"Okay, so the edge of the heart points that way." Becky turned in the saddle, pointing off across the way. "I was thinking we should ride in that direction until we reach the moors, then look for a likely spot that matches the rest of the description."

"Makes sense," Winnie agreed.

Mia frowned. "Not really, actually."

"Do you have a better idea?" Zoe asked her. "No? Me neither. So let's go!"

"I still think we should have kept going," Becky said as the group rode into the stable yard a couple of hours later. "There's that cove just like a twenty-minute ride farther than we went . . ."

"No way," Mia said. "I fulfilled the dare. And I'm hungry. I want my lunch."

Zoe had to admit that her stomach was grumbling, too. Searching the moors under the warm sun had made her hungry. "Who wants to come to Grandpa's place for sandwiches?" she offered.

"Thanks, but I brought a lunch," Mia said, while Winnie, Heather, and Becky said they had, too.

In the end, Aaron, Jade, and Gaby were the only ones who went home with Zoe. "Let's bring our sandwiches back to the stables, though," Aaron suggested. "Then we can eat with the others."

Twenty minutes later, they were hurrying back into the yard with sandwiches and drinks. Mia had disappeared, but Becky and the Breakfast Club were in the courtyard sitting on upturned buckets eating their lunch. Marcus was nearby piling hay into a wheelbarrow.

Becky glanced up when Zoe and the others appeared. "Come look at this," she called. "I was just going over the latest footage and I found something odd."

"What is it?" Zoe took a bite of her sandwich and headed over to look over her friend's shoulder.

"Just here—look." Becky pointed at the screen. "It's when we first ride up beside Twisted Beech Wood, see?

Raven is jumping around, and Princess keeps staring into the trees."

Zoe nodded. Heather's pony was clearly visible on-screen, her ears pricked.

"So what's she looking at, I wonder?" Jade said, looking over Becky's other shoulder. "And don't say it's a ghost."

"I'm not saying a word. But look." Becky fast-forwarded slightly, then pointed again.

Zoe leaned closer. "There's something there, just barely visible in the corner," she said. "It looks white— and it's about the size of that dog I saw . . ."

"You saw a dog?" Becky sat up straight and spun around to face her. "When? Where? Was it Peter the Young's ghost dog?"

Zoe held up her hands, laughing. "I don't know," she said. "I took that shortcut when I went to see Pin after dinner yesterday. Raven spooked again and then something dashed past us—it looked like a dog, but it was pretty dark and I didn't get a good look . . ."

"Ghost dog!" Becky's eyes went wide. "I knew it! And we just caught it on film. This is great!"

At that moment Mia emerged from the stable office with Susie at her heels. "Hey, what happened?" Zoe asked Susie. "I thought you were going shopping."

"My mum had to reschedule." Susie shrugged. "So what's happening with the game? Are we still playing?"

"Bobsolutely!" Becky said. "Our ice-cream dare is getting mega hits! Just give me a sec to post the brooch hunt, and then it's your turn, Mia."

Mia looked bored. "Whatever. Truth or dare, Zoe."

"Wait!" Becky squawked. "I said give me a sec . . ." She fiddled with the camera for a moment. Then she handed it back to Aaron. "Okay—go!"

Mia sighed loudly. "Truth or dare, Zoe?"

"Truth—always," Zoe replied. It was her usual response when playing Truth or Dare, but this time Becky looked disappointed.

"Are you sure you don't want to choose dare, Zoe?" she said. "It would be more fun. For the viewers, I mean."

Zoe shrugged. "Sorry. I'm sure Mia can come up with something *fun* to ask me."

"Sure, if you want to play it safe . . ." Gaby murmured.

Zoe ignored her. "Well, Mia? Ask me anything."

"Ask her what color her underpants are," Aaron called out. "Because I see her laundry, and she's got some crazy ones!"

Zoe laughed. "No repeats," she said. "You have to come up with something new, Mia."

"Just don't ask her which horse in the stables is her

favorite," Jade joked. "I think we all know the answer to that one."

That made everyone laugh—except Mia. She looked thoughtful.

"Okay, I've got it," she said. "Zoe, answer truthfully—if you suddenly had to fly off back to America, which person out of anyone who's here right now"—she waved a hand at the group—"would you want to ride and take care of Raven while you're gone?"

Becky and Jade traded a look. "One person?" Becky asked. "Or can it be more than one?"

"Yeah, what about two people working as a team?" Jade added.

"Or even three," Aaron said.

Zoe hardly heard them as she thought about Mia's question. She loved Raven with all her heart, but she was the first to admit he wasn't always easy to deal with—or to ride. Their bond made it seem easy, but anyone else would have their hands full.

"How long would I have to leave him?" she asked Mia. "Like, a few days, or months and months?"

Mia shook her head. "Irrelevant. Just answer the question."

Zoe took a deep breath. The question was more important than she let on. It was something on her mind a lot lately—if she were to leave, what would happen to Raven? Of course, she planned to take him with her if she made it onto the US team, but Raven was fragile; he'd been through so much. Would he handle the journey overseas? Or would he be happier staying here at Bright Fields?

Zoe wished Pin was there—she knew he'd do anything for her; plus, he was the best rider she knew. He'd be able and willing to handle Raven for sure. She glanced at Marcus, knowing he could handle it, too. But then she shook her head. Marcus was busy running the stables. If she was being honest . . .

"Gaby," she blurted out, almost before she knew she was going to say it. "I'd trust Gaby to do it."

Gaby raised her eyebrows. "Okay, I didn't expect that," she said.

"Neither did I," Becky muttered.

Zoe looked around. Becky and Jade were frowning. Aaron looked a little bit sad. Even Marcus seemed confused by her answer.

"Listen, guys," she said. "It's nothing against anyone else—I know I could trust any of you. It's just, you know, Gaby—"

"Whatever, doesn't matter," Jade broke in. "It's your turn to pick someone, Zoe."

Zoe hesitated. Had Jade and Becky expected her to

choose them because they'd been friends longer? But that wasn't really the point, was it? The game called for the truth . . .

"Can't think of someone to ask?" Mia checked her watch. "Too bad. Come on, Susie, let's go get some frozen yogurt or something."

"No!" Becky cried. "Wait, the game's not over. Mia's question for Zoe was, um, kind of boring. We should try to fit in at least one more interesting thing we can post."

"Fine." If Becky was going to ignore the tension, Zoe decided she would, too. "Um . . . Jade. Truth or dare?"

"Truth," Jade said. Glancing at Becky, she shrugged. "Sorry. I'm not really in the mood for a dare right now."

Zoe frowned. Jade still sounded weird. "Okay, truth it is," Zoe said. Come to think of it, maybe she *wasn't* ready to ignore the tension after all . . . "Jade, tell the truth— why are you acting upset right now?"

"I'm not acting upset," Jade retorted.

"You have to tell the truth," Heather said. "You *do* seem a bit weird all of a sudden."

"Yeah, all right, you're right." Jade put her hands on her hips and stared at Zoe. "It's really not a huge deal, okay? But here's the truth. I'm kind of upset because Zoe sometimes acts like she forgets all about me—us." She shot a look toward Becky.

"What?" Zoe cried. "Jade, please—I didn't mean it that way! You're taking this way out of context."

"No, she's not," Becky said. "Jade and I were the first ones to believe in you and Raven. But now I guess you think we're not good enough for him. Or for you."

"But that's not what I meant," Zoe protested. "Seriously, if you'd just let me explain . . ."

"No," Jade cut her off sharply. "No explanations. Not right now." She glanced toward Aaron, who was still filming.

Zoe looked that way, too. Her cousin stared back, not smiling.

Annoyance and frustration bubbled up inside Zoe, too fast to stop it. Why wouldn't anyone let her *explain*?

"Okay, Jade, I guess it's your turn," Susie said brightly, as if nothing was happening.

"Right," Jade said. "I think I'll ask, um . . ."

"Excuse me." Zoe got up. "I—I really need to get out of here right now."

Not waiting to see if anyone tried to stop her, she hurried out of the yard and ran toward home.

Zoe's grandfather, Frank, wandered into the cluttered farmhouse kitchen. Zoe was sitting at the table staring at her phone.

"You're home early, Zoe," Frank said kindly. "Anything wrong?"

"Only everything." Zoe sighed and forced a smile for her grandfather. "Just kidding—sort of. Becky has us all playing this silly online game of Truth or Dare, and, well, here." She held up her phone. "See for yourself. She posted another video after I left."

"Ah, yes, Aaron told me about the game when you were here for lunch. He seemed rather excited." Frank leaned over for a better look as Zoe pushed Play. The video showed the latest dare—Jade had dared Susie to try riding with a purple wig on.

Frank smiled. "A purple wig? Sounds like a circus trick."

"It is, mostly." Zoe turned her gaze back to the video as Marcus brought out Casper, one of Bright Fields's quietest and smallest ponies.

"Here's the horse. Well? Where's the wig?" Marcus asked dubiously.

"Oh, would you look at that!" Susie said. "If there's no wig, I guess I can't do the dare. Silly me."

Jade took out a silky purple wig from her knapsack. "Think again," she said. Then, on the group's bemused look, "Don't ask me why I had this, but also, don't pretend you're mad I do."

Heather laughed. "I have so many questions!"

Zoe watched as Jade tied Susie's hair back and put the wig on. Seeing Susie in the crazy wig reminded Zoe of the time Susie had accidentally dyed her hair the exact same shade. She looked edgy, cool even. Susie had a habit of making everything look effortless. Susie strapped on her helmet. Her long, purple locks were flowing from underneath it.

On the screen, Susie took a deep breath, then vaulted onto Casper's back. "Here goes nothing," she said with a laugh.

Then, while riding Casper, she struck a pose.

"Wow, very impressive," Frank said as he watched.

Zoe nodded, holding her breath, even though she'd

already seen the video a couple of times and knew what happened next.

Susie had gotten too invested in the situation. She was now taking it upon herself to strike even wilder poses. She flung her hair back and forth, then she took her hands off the horse and pretended to use an end of the purple hair as a mustache.

Wham! The tricks were too much. Susie fell off.

Frank winced. "Oh, dear!"

"Don't worry, she's all right—see?" Zoe watched as Susie stood up, brushing dirt off her jods. As the onlookers cheered, Susie grinned and curtsied.

"That was kind of fun!" she exclaimed, stepping over to give Casper a pat.

Zoe hit Stop on the video, which paused on a still shot of Susie's enthusiastic audience—with Becky and Jade front and center. Zoe stared at their faces, feeling confused and distressed about what had happened earlier. It wasn't like either of them to fly off the handle like that. Had she really hurt their feelings that much by choosing Gaby?

Meanwhile, Frank still looked concerned. "These dares are encouraging bad behavior," he said.

"Marcus wouldn't let us do anything too crazy," Zoe cut him off, more concerned about furious friends than dangerous dares. "Listen, Grandpa, I think I'd better go back." Pocketing her phone, she paused just long enough to give him a peck on the cheek. "See you later for dinner, okay?"

The yard was quiet when Zoe arrived; the only living thing in sight was a bird pecking at some hay chaff on the ground. Zoe stopped and glanced around.

"Where is everybody?" she said to herself out loud.

Suddenly, Winnie's pigtailed head popped out of a stall. "Zoe—you're back!"

"I'm back," Zoe confirmed. "What happened to everyone else?"

Winnie stepped out of the stall holding a pitchfork. "Mia and I just had a little chat about advice and such. Mia got sick of playing, so she and Susie went off somewhere," she said. "Marcus is teaching a lesson to some adults in the arena, and I think Gaby's helping him set jumps or something. Aaron and Heather went to dump the wheelbarrow. Oh, and I think Jecky's in the hayloft."

Jecky—that was what Jade and Becky sometimes called themselves when they were together. Usually Zoe loved the name, but right now it made her feel a little left out.

Left out—like the two of them felt when I chose Gaby over them? she wondered.

"Thanks, Winnie," she said. "I think I'd better go find, um, Jecky."

"See if they want to keep playing Truth or Dare," Winnie said hopefully. "I know Aaron and Heather want to get more videos."

"We'll see." With a smile for the younger girl, Zoe headed off toward the hayloft.

Becky and Jade were bent over Becky's phone when Zoe climbed up to join them. Jade's eyes were wary as she glanced up.

"Oh, um, hi, Zoe," she said. "Where'd you run off to in such a hurry earlier?"

"Never mind that," Zoe said. "I was thinking—Becky, how about another treasure-hunting trip? I'm in the mood for a ride on the moors right now."

Becky's face brightened. "Really? That's a horse-some idea, Zoe!" she said. "I mean, I still think we should have gone a bit farther this morning, but Mia was griping so much . . ."

"I'm in, too." Jade still looked cautious, but she shot Zoe a small smile. "Let's go get the horses ready."

Ten minutes later Raven, Bob, and Major were tacked up. Zoe swung into the saddle and waited for her friends to do the same. Then all three of them rode toward the exit.

They were almost there when all three members of the Breakfast Club came running. "Where are you going?" Heather cried.

"I thought we were going to play some more after Marcus finished his lesson," Winnie added.

"We can pick up the game later," Becky said. "Better yet, you guys go ahead without us. Just upload anything good, okay?"

The girls looked uncertain, but Aaron nodded. "You got it," he said. "I have some great ideas for new dares!"

"Great. Just be careful, okay?" Zoe said, remembering her grandfather's comment. "Don't do anything I wouldn't do."

Waving at the younger kids, she aimed Raven toward the lane. As soon as they left the yard, Jade looked over at her. "Zoe, listen, about earlier . . ."

"No, I was just about to start." Zoe took a deep breath. "I'm really sorry, you two. You know I trust you guys more than, well, pretty much anyone in the entire world, right? I wasn't thinking when I picked Gaby for that truth."

"Sure you were," Jade countered with a small smile. "You knew she could handle Raven better than we could."

"Yeah. Riding Raven would be a big shock after being

so used to Bob." Becky patted her horse. "Your crazy horse would probably dump me in the dirt as soon as I swung a leg over."

Zoe laughed. "No way. You're both great riders—way better than you give yourselves credit for." She shrugged. "I just thought Gaby deserved the chance—"

"Never mind, Zoe. You don't have to explain." Jade reached across the space between their horses and squeezed her arm. "We probably overreacted."

"Speak for yourself," Becky told Jade. "I wasn't that upset, really."

"Really?" Jade cocked an eyebrow. "Truth or dare, Becky . . ."

"Okay, okay." Becky grinned. "Maybe I was a *little* insulted. But now I think about it, I've got my hands full with Bob. Him and Raven together? Trouble."

"With a capital T," Zoe agreed with a grin. She shot a sidelong look at her friends, wanting to finish what she'd started to say. But they seemed happy now, so maybe it wasn't that important . . .

"Anyway, I'm sorry, too, Zoe," Jade said. "I know I didn't let you explain before. But I realized the camera was still going, and it really didn't seem like a discussion to have in front of the world, and . . ."

"I know," Zoe said. "It's okay. Really." She looked

from Jade to Becky. "Best Friends Forever?"

"Best Friends Forever!" her friends chorused.

And with that, everything was back to normal. Discussion turned to their brooch hunt. Becky had several new theories about where to look for the spot mentioned in the book.

"There's that hilly bit near the stream that looks sort of like a heart," she said. "That covers the sound of water thing, too."

"I thought it was the 'voice of the sea'?" Jade said.

Becky shrugged. "That's probably just poetic license. Anyway, that spot's pretty close to the cliffs overlooking the sea, so maybe it's near enough? Worth a look, anyhow."

"For sure," Zoe agreed. "Especially since it's pretty close to here."

She rode Raven off the trail and across a small gully. Jade followed, with Becky and Bob bringing up the rear.

As Bob clambered up the bank on the far side of the gully, Becky snapped her fingers. "Almost forgot," she said. "I wanted to ask Pin if he knows anything more about Peter the Young. Maybe if we knew more about him, it'd give us a hint as to where to search."

"I'm not sure Pin knows that much about any of his ancestors." Zoe pulled her phone out of her pocket with one hand, hanging on to the reins with the other. "But maybe he could ask Arthur—that guy knows just about everything about the dukes, right? I'll text Pin right now."

She tapped out the message with one hand: *Becky wants to know if u know stuff about peter the young that might help find the brooch*

"Thanks," Becky said. They crossed through a forested area that separated the coastline from the central moors, and as they emerged from the trees, rolling curves of green and amber grasses stretched out as far as they could see.

Zoe took a deep breath as a breeze brought her a whiff of wildflowers. "Sometimes I forget how beautiful this place is," she said.

Jade smiled. "Anyone fancy a canter?"

Half an hour later, the trio had slowed to a walk to let the horses rest. Zoe and Raven were in the lead as they crested an especially high hill. "We're almost to that spot," she called over her shoulder. "We should be able to see the stream from up . . ." Her voice trailed off as Raven stopped at the top. "Oh, weird," she blurted out at the sight that greeted her from halfway across the next valley.

"What is it?" Jade called, urging Major on faster. "Do you see something?"

"Is it the ghost dog?" Becky exclaimed eagerly, nudging

Bob into a lumbering canter to catch up. "Or a hint to the treasure?"

"Not exactly." Zoe clutched the reins, wondering if she was seeing things.

By now Jade had seen what she'd seen. "Not the ghost dog—just a couple of riders," she said, squinting at the tiny figures. "What's so weird about that?"

Becky was peering at the riders, too. "It's Alex and Susie!"

"Oh," Jade said. "Okay, that is weird."

"Right. Especially since Alex told me he was going home because his horse was tired." Becky frowned slightly. "So what's he doing way out here, on that very same horse—and with Susie of all people?"

"Yeah, I thought she went off somewhere with Mia." Jade shrugged. "Guess not . . ."

It was pretty clear that Alex and Susie didn't realize anyone else was around. They were riding at the walk, their horses side by side.

Zoe gulped, remembering Gaby's comments when they'd seen Alex with Susie before. Was she right? Was there some kind of secret romance going on behind Becky's back?

No! Zoe thought. *Alex wouldn't do that to Becky . . . Would he?*

Zoe could tell Becky was confused, too, but before she could talk to her about it, her phone pinged. "The Breakfast Club just posted another video," Becky said eagerly, moving on with the conversation. "Let's check it out!"

She slid down from Bob's back, and Jade dismounted, too. Zoe glanced once more toward Alex and Susie—just in time to see their horses disappear behind a copse of trees. Then she swung down from Raven's back, pulling the reins over his head so he could graze.

"Okay, let's see what those crazy kids are up to now," Zoe said, leaning in for a better look at Becky's screen.

The three of them watched as Becky pressed Play. The video began with Heather daring Aaron to take a selfie in the muck heap. That seemed easy enough—until she held up a pair of silly mustache-and-glasses masks.

"And you have to wear these!" Heather finished with a grin.

"Where'd she get those?" Zoe wondered as they watched Aaron grab one of the masks out of Winnie's hand and stick it on his own face. "Everyone has such interesting things."

"Who knows—maybe that souvenir stand at the pier," Jade said. "Better question: Who's filming this?"

"I don't know." Becky tilted her head as the camera suddenly turned sideways. "But I think I'm getting seasick."

On-screen, Heather frowned into the camera. "Keep it steady, Gaby!" she chided.

"Look, if you're going to be such a critic, you can film it yourself," Gaby's voice said from offscreen.

Jade laughed. "I guess it's good that she's there," she commented. "One member of the Pony Squad needs to have their eyes on the dares at all times."

Zoe nodded. The footage cut out for a second, and when it resumed, Aaron was in the muck heap.

Soon the entire Pony Squad was laughing as Aaron knelt down into the muck heap. The edges of his pants got messy and muddy. Then he dipped a hand into the water and pretended to splash it onto Susie.

"Is someone afraid of mud?" Aaron said, laughing. He kept splashing the muck at Susie, who howled with laughter.

"Afraid? You'll see," she said. Then she plopped right in it, up to her torso!

"Ew! Susie!" Heather called.

"It's fun," Susie shot back. "Come on. Join us. I *dare* you."

Heather smiled. Then she entered the muck, too.

"It doesn't count unless we take a selfie," Heather said. The trio took a photo of themselves in the mud (Aaron wore his sunglasses) and then got out. "Now we need a shower."

As the trio hosed themselves off, Heather announced, "Dare completed! We'll post the selfie separately on the vlog. In the meantime, it's your turn to choose, Aaron."

Aaron turned and grinned into the camera. Gaby's voice rang out again: "Don't even think about picking me, kid," she warned.

"Fine." Aaron rolled his eyes. "Winnie—truth or dare?"

The camera turned to focus on Winnie. She looked a little nervous. "Um, I guess . . ."

"Come on, Winnie," Heather said. "Choose dare!"

"Okay." Winnie straightened her shoulders. She hadn't yet completed a dare yet. This was finally her chance to prove herself. "Dare!"

"Hmm, what should I dare her to do?" Aaron grinned into the camera. "Maybe spend the night alone in super-spoooooooky Twisted Beech Wood?" He wiggled his fingers in a ghostly way.

"What? No!" Winnie exclaimed in horror. "I mean—if that's what everyone else is doing."

"You can't do that—it'd take too long," Heather pointed out.

Aaron shrugged. "Guess you're right. But I really wanted to dare her to face a ghost . . . I know!" He grinned again. "Winnie, I dare you to look for that ghost dog Becky told us about—by riding as close as you can get to the edge of Moonlight Cliff!"

*W*hen Zoe galloped into the yard a few minutes later, the entire Breakfast Club was perched on the hitching rail. Gaby was using a pitchfork to toss straw into a stall nearby.

"Oh, thank goodness!" Zoe cried breathlessly, flinging herself out of the saddle and yanking off her helmet. "Winnie, you can't ride along the edge of Moonlight Cliff. It's way too dangerous! Only a skilled rider could do that."

Gaby rolled her eyes. "You're a little late, Zoe. I told them the same thing like fifteen minutes ago."

"You did?" Zoe was a little surprised. Gaby wasn't usually the type to play the responsible adult. "Okay, good. And we got back here as fast as we could, by the way."

Just then Major cantered into view, followed by Bob. "Are they still here?" Jade called worriedly.

"Don't worry, Winnie chickened out even before Gaby said anything," Aaron told the older girls with a snort. He glanced at Zoe's horse, who was sweaty and a bit wild-eyed after the headlong gallop across the moors. "I mean, it's not like I dared her to ride Raven or something. That would've been reckless."

Winnie dropped her head, staring at her paddock boots without saying a word. "Aaron!" Zoe exclaimed, hurrying over to put an arm around the younger girl's shoulders. "That's not a very nice thing to say. Friends don't say stuff like that—and if they do accidentally say something stupid, they apologize." She shot a quick smile toward Becky and Jade, then turned to glare at her cousin. "Tell Winnie you're sorry!"

"I am," Aaron said quickly, taking a step toward Winnie. "I was just kidding around, but I guess it came out wrong. Sorry, Winnie."

"Yeah, it was a silly dare, anyhow," Heather said. "It would be way hard to film something like that and make it look exciting. Come on, Aaron, give her a better one. Or maybe a truth would be better."

"No," Winnie said. "I—I don't feel like playing anymore right now, okay? You can pick someone else. I guess

I wasn't meant to be part of this. Zoe, why don't you film for a bit? I'm going to get a drink of water."

Zoe took the camera. "Yeah, how about Gaby?" she said. "She hasn't had a turn yet."

"Sorry," Gaby said, not sounding very sorry at all. "I told Marcus I'd finish bedding the stalls before his lesson is over." She dropped her pitchfork in a wheelbarrow and pushed it off down the shed row.

"Okay, how about one of you?" Aaron rubbed his hands, glancing from Zoe to her friends.

"Count me out." Becky checked her phone from atop Bob's back. "Did Pin text you back yet, Zoe? If not, I might ride over there and talk to him in person."

Zoe checked her phone. "Nope, nothing yet."

"Okay, then I'm off." Becky tossed them all a salute. "May the Bob be with you." With that, she rode toward the exit.

Jade slid down from Major's saddle. "Don't pick me, either, Aaron," she said, giving the sweaty horse a pat. "I have to give this guy a bath. He worked hard trying to keep up with Raven."

"How about you, Zoe?" Aaron said. "Truth or dare?"

"Nope, I'm out, too," Zoe said. "I have to untack Raven. Besides, I just had a turn, remember?"

"But there's no one else!" her cousin complained. "I'm

not allowed to ask Heather, since she gave me the last official dare."

Zoe shrugged. "Is that all? I hereby order an exception to the rule," she said with a dramatic wave of one hand. "Go ahead and ask Heather, if she's okay with that."

Heather was, and she chose dare. Zoe tied Raven to the hitching rail and listened as she pulled off his saddle. Then Winnie came back from her water break. Zoe noticed her eyes seemed a little puffy but she didn't say anything. Winnie filmed Aaron as he strode back and forth, dramatically pondering his decision.

"Got it!" he said at last, stopping in front of Heather. "Here's your dare. You have to dress up in a business suit and ride Princess to the mayor's office building." He grinned. "And then you have to tell the receptionist that you're there for an important meeting. And that you and Princess switched places, and Princess is actually you and you're Princess."

Winnie laughed quietly. "That's perfect!" she exclaimed. "Your mum will think it's hilarious, Heather!"

Zoe wasn't so sure about that. The mayor didn't seem to have such a great sense of humor as far as she could tell. Still, Heather was the mayor's daughter. What was the worst that could happen?

Jade looked up from hosing Major, her expression worried. "Are you sure that's a good idea?" she called. "The town hall is right in, well, town—do you know if Princess is traffic safe?"

"Oh!" Heather frowned. "I hadn't thought of that. I mean, I've only had her a short while . . ."

"It'll be okay," Zoe assured her. She glanced at Jade. "We can ride along with them just in case, okay?"

"Thanks, Zoe." Heather looked relieved. "Then I'll do it!"

Zoe and Jade finished cooling out their horses and then tacked them up again. "Poor Major," Jade commented. "And here I'd just promised him a nice rest and some hay . . ."

"This shouldn't take long." Zoe checked the time on her phone. "I hope they're almost ready, though. I told Pin I'd try to stop by before dinnertime to help with the cleaning."

Half an hour later, Zoe pulled Raven to a halt and glanced behind her. She couldn't help smiling at what she saw. Heather looked ridiculous! She didn't own a business suit, not a proper one anyway, so Aaron had run home to Grandpa's house, where he'd found an oversized business suit left over from a costume party. Heather gave a thumbs-up and wore it valiantly. Meanwhile, she had brushed Princess's tail extra nice to make her look spiffy. And to top it all off, she had a handful of hay in her pocket, which no one was really sure why, but Heather promised it would be extra video-worthy.

"Here we are," Zoe said, waving a hand at the impressive facade of the town hall. "Are you guys ready?"

Aaron held up the camera. "I am!"

"Me too." Winnie lifted her phone. "We're going to film from two angles—Aaron says he can edit it to look really cool afterward!"

"I'm ready, too." Heather squared her shoulders, looking nervous. "I hope my mum doesn't get too cross . . ."

Aaron lowered the camera. "Uh-uh, no way, you can't chicken out now!" he exclaimed. He made some loud chicken noises, which spooked Raven slightly.

"Stop it, Aaron," Zoe told him, quickly getting her horse back under control. "It's not nice to tease your friends." She glanced at Winnie, who was staring down at her phone with an anxious expression. Did she think Aaron was making fun of her, too, because of the earlier dare? Zoe was pretty sure he wasn't—her cousin didn't hold grudges like that. She just hoped Winnie knew that.

Meanwhile, Jade was watching the traffic, which was light at that time of the afternoon. "Let's hurry up and cross while it's safe," she said. "We can tie the other horses outside—I'll stay with them if you like."

"Thanks, Jade." Zoe urged Raven forward, his hooves clip-clopping on the pavement.

Halfway across, she heard her phone ping. It was a text from Pin:

Just saw your text. Why are you asking about P the Y? And what brooch do you mean?

Aaron, Winnie, Heather, and Jade had dismounted by then. Jade was bustling around, making sure all the horses were tied securely. "Coming, Zoe?" Winnie called.

"In a sec—I just need to text Pin back," Zoe replied, a little distracted.

Zoe quickly tapped out her response to Pin: *Will tell you when I see you in a bit. Isn't Becky there yet?*

She hit Send, then looked up. Heather had already disappeared inside.

"Better hurry," Jade said with a smile. "You don't want to miss this, right?"

"Right." Zoe pocketed her phone and pushed in through the door.

Heather was standing in front of the reception desk. She was talking to the startled-looking young man behind the desk as her friends filmed.

"No. You don't understand. *I* am the horse," Heather said, trying to convince the receptionist. She gestured outside, where Princess was safely tied up. "My rider and I switched places, and I—"

"That's utter hogwash!" the receptionist exclaimed, flapping his hands.

"I already told you, I have a very important meeting with the mayor!" Heather told him in a haughty voice. "She's the only one that can help me! *Neigh!*"

The young man narrowed his eyes and leaned forward. "Hang on—aren't you the mayor's kid?" he said. "Hannah, right?"

"It's Heather," Winnie corrected him. "But as you can see, that's not Heather. That's Princess."

And then, as if to prove that she was really Princess, Heather took the handful of hay out of her pocket and took a big, delicious bite. Aaron whooped with laughter.

At that moment, there was a clatter of footsteps on the stairs beyond the desk. The mayor herself appeared— and stopped short, taking in the scene before her.

"Heather!" she snapped after a moment. "What on earth are you doing here?"

Heather gulped. There were still a few stray pieces of hay dangling from her mouth. "Er, hello, Mum."

The mayor was not enthused. She looked from Heather to Winnie to Zoe and sighed.

"Okay, maybe we'd better get out of here now," Heather said, laughing.

"Hang on a moment!" The mayor glared at Heather. "First, we need to talk . . ."

❧

"What happened?" Jade asked as the group filed out of the town hall a few minutes later.

"What *didn't* happen?" Aaron lifted his camera and grinned. "This video is going to be *epic*!"

Heather sighed. "My mum came down and had a whole conversation about human and horse nutrition," she told Jade. "It was so epic I'm banned from playing Truth or Dare for the rest of my life."

"Oh, dear." Jade shook her head sympathetically.

"Yeah, that could've gone better," Zoe said. She checked her phone. Pin had texted back saying he hadn't seen Becky all day. "Hmm, that's weird . . ." she murmured. She looked up at Jade. "Becky never arrived at the castle."

"That *is* weird." Jade frowned. "I'll try calling her."

But there was no answer. Zoe checked Raven's girth, then swung into the saddle. "We'd better go check on her," she told Jade. Then she glanced at the younger kids. "If we take you as far as the Castle Road, can you ride back to Bright Fields on your own?"

"Of course," Aaron said. The two girls nodded.

"Good." Jade gathered Major's reins and mounted. "Then let's go."

A short while later, Zoe and Jade rode onto the castle grounds. There was no sign of Becky or Bob, though Pin was there saddling his horse, Elvis.

He looked up as Zoe and Jade trotted toward him. "I figured you'd want to ride out to look for Becky, since she seems to be missing," he told them.

"We do." Zoe halted Raven and glanced around. "It's weird that she's not answering her phone."

"Maybe she dropped it," Jade suggested. "Or Bob ate it?"

Zoe smiled. "Possible. But I'll feel better when we find her."

"Why was she coming here, anyway?" Pin asked. "And what's all this about treasure?"

Zoe and Jade quickly filled him in about the legend of

Peter the Young. "So you know Becky," Zoe finished with a smile. "She's planning to find that brooch so you can add it to your tremendous Dukely fortune." She winked. "And maybe you'll even give her a reward to add to her non-dukely non-fortune."

Pin grimaced. "I see," he said. "Well, I hate to break it to her, but—"

Before he could finish, a bloodcurdling scream rang out from the forest nearby.

9

*W*hat was that?" Zoe cried, hanging on as Raven spun around, snorting at the sudden noise. Even Major and Elvis were on high alert, ears pricked and nostrils flared as they stared toward the forest.

"Let's find out." Pin vaulted into the saddle and rode toward the trees.

Zoe and Jade followed. All three horses were still a few strides from the forest when a lone figure burst into view.

"Becky!" Zoe cried, pulling Raven to a sudden halt.

A second later, Bob wandered out behind his owner. He glanced briefly at the other horses, then lowered his head to nibble at the grass.

Jade jumped down from the saddle. "Was that you screaming?" she cried. "What's wrong? Did you fall off Bob? Are you hurt?"

"No, I'm fine." Becky shook her head, looking slightly sheepish. "But listen—I think I just heard the ghost dog barking!"

Zoe glanced toward the trees, remembering that white creature she'd seen the previous evening, and the white blur on the video earlier that day. "You did?"

"Uh-huh." Becky nodded so vigorously that her braids bounced. "I was on my way here"—she waved a hand toward the castle—"and decided to take the shortcut through Twisted Beech Wood. I was thinking about that branch that's shaped like a heart—"

"Well, sort of," Jade murmured.

Becky ignored her. "So I thought, what if it's not pointing toward the moors after all? What if it's a clue that the treasure is buried right there in the spooky haunted wood?"

"But it said it was on the moors," Jade pointed out.

Pin rolled his eyes. "And the wood isn't haunted," he added. "Besides—"

"Anyway, I got off to check a likely treasure-hiding spot, and that's when the ghost dog tried to attack Bob."

"It attacked Bob?" Jade glanced at the stout cob, who was still grazing. "He doesn't look very upset."

Becky shrugged. "Bob's not scared of ghosts, I guess. Anyway, I heard something that sounded like a bark, and when I shouted, it ran away. Unfortunately, I'd turned off my camera, so I didn't get any footage this time. But I bet if we go back right now, we could find it again!"

Zoe traded an amused look with Jade and Pin. "Shall we?"

"I suppose so," Jade said. "Everyone's seen this ghost so far except me—I'm feeling left out."

"I haven't seen it, either," Pin reminded her. "Not that it actually exists . . ."

Still, he rode along as the three girls mounted and rode toward the forest. Becky led the way, her phone at the ready with the video camera on.

"It was just here," she said, halting Bob in the center of a clearing. "I was over there, and—"

A sudden flurry of barking cut her off. Zoe spun in the saddle just in time to see a small, fluffy white dog race out and leap toward Major's hind legs, yapping all the while.

"Easy, boy!" Jade cried as the horse spun around, snorting with alarm.

Just then a girl of about five ran out of the forest. "Puffball, stop!" she cried. "I'm sorry—he's just trying to be friendly . . ."

A woman burst into view behind the girl. Zoe recognized her immediately—it was Bea, the young woman from Imogen's cleaning team!

"Is that your dog?" Zoe called, hanging on to the reins as Raven backed away from the little dog.

"I'm sorry—yes!" Bea replied breathlessly. "Puffball, come here, you little rascal . . ."

She and the young girl circled around and finally managed to trap the dog between them. Bea caught him and picked him up.

The horses calmed down quickly once the puppy wasn't racing around underfoot. Becky rode Bob closer to Bea, peering at the pup in her arms. "It's not a ghost dog," she said, sounding slightly disappointed. "It's a real one!"

"Yes, this is our Puffball," Bea said, looking confused by Becky's comment. "Imogen got him for us to help convince me and Trixie to come to the island for this project." She glanced at the little girl, who was staring up at Raven in awe.

"Is that your horse?" Trixie said. "He's beautiful!"

"Thanks." Zoe smiled and dismounted. Then she led Raven closer. "You can pet his nose if you want," she offered. "He won't mind."

Raven lowered his head and snuffled at the little girl's outstretched hand. "Oh, his nose is so soft!" Trixie exclaimed. "Mama, will Miss Imogen get us a horse next time?"

That made everyone laugh. "Your dog is awfully cute, though," Jade said.

"Cute, yes, but also quite naughty," Bea said with a rueful smile. "Every time someone opens the cottage door, he races out wanting to explore. I'm sorry if he scared your horses."

"It's all right." Becky slid down from Bob's back. "Can I pet him?"

For the next few minutes, Zoe was pretty sure nobody thought about treasure or ghosts or anything else. Trixie took turns patting all the horses, then gasped when Becky offered to give her a pony ride on Bob. After that, Puffball the puppy got a turn, standing balanced on Bob's saddle while Zoe led him around and Becky filmed the whole thing.

Finally, Bea said she had to get back to fixing dinner. She, Trixie, and Puffball left after more pats and good-byes and a few excited barks.

"So much for Peter the Young's spooky ghost dog," Zoe said as she watched them disappear into the forest. She glanced at Pin.

"Silver lining, right?" Becky shrugged. "At least we got a cute video out of it." She played back the clip of the little dog "riding" Bob. "Adorable! I'll post it later. Right now I'll just send it to Alex—he loves dogs."

She did so. Then she waited, staring at her phone, clearly expecting an immediate reply.

"Give it a moment, Becky," Jade said with a smile. "Maybe he's busy."

"No, he always checks messages right away." Becky chewed her lower lip, a shadow of worry crossing her face. "Especially when they involve cute dogs . . ."

"Never mind," Zoe said quickly, flashing back to Gaby's suspicions about Alex and Susie, and then to the sighting of the pair earlier on the moors. Maybe Gaby had been too quick to jump to conclusions. But even Zoe had to admit that there seemed to be something odd going on . . . Luckily she knew the perfect topic to distract Becky from thinking too much about that. "What about Peter the Young's treasure?" she blurted out. "Any new leads?"

"Not really," Becky said. "I got a little distracted by Puffball the Friendly Ghost."

Pin cleared his throat. "Actually, I've been trying to tell you," he said. "That brooch from the picture in the book? It's not actually lost."

All three girls turned to stare at him. "It's not?" Zoe said. "What do you mean?"

"I mean it's safe and sound in the castle right now." Pin shrugged and shoved his hands in his pockets. "Arthur showed the brooch to me."

"Oh." Becky blinked. "Wait. So the brooch isn't the buried treasure?"

"I guess not," Jade said. "That was just a guess, wasn't it?"

Becky nodded, her disappointed expression going thoughtful. "So if the brooch isn't the treasure, what could it be? Maybe something even more fabulous!"

Pin smiled slightly. "I have no idea," he said. "But Arthur told me Peter the Young didn't care much about jewels and such. In that portrait, his hand is on the brooch because he wanted to take it off."

"Wow, Arthur knows a lot about your ancestors, doesn't he?" Zoe commented.

"Yeah." Pin chuckled. "It's a bit spooky, actually. Oh! Speaking of spooky, he also said Peter the Young loved looking out over that cliff. It was his favorite spot on the island."

Becky gasped. "Moonlight Cliff? We haven't searched there yet!"

"I guess hanging out in that spot runs in the family," Jade said.

Zoe smiled. "It must—I know it's one of your favorite places to ride, Pin."

"Less talk, more action." Becky grabbed her stirrup and swung onto Bob's back. "We have to go check it out!"

"But it's getting late," Jade protested. "I'll be expected home for dinner soon."

"It's not that late," Becky argued. "There are hours yet

until—" She cut herself off as her phone pinged. "Maybe that's Alex!" Her face fell slightly when she checked the screen. "No, it's the Breakfast Club. They just posted another dare." Her eyes widened. "They're at the Firefly Hotel!"

"What are they doing there?" Zoe asked, surprised. "They must have turned around and ridden right over there after we left them!"

"I guess." Becky squinted at the small phone screen. "Oh my Bob—someone dared Gaby to make a ruckus in the hotel lobby, and now that scary Geoff guy is threatening to call the police!"

Zoe gasped. "What should we do?"

"What *can* we do?" Jade exclaimed. "I knew this game was going to get someone in real trouble!"

Pin sighed. "Never mind," he said, stepping over to swing into Elvis's saddle. "I'll take care of it. But only if you all promise to end this silly Truth or Dare thing."

"You?" Becky sounded surprised.

He shot them all a small smile as he urged his horse into motion. "There are some advantages to being a duke, I suppose," he called over his shoulder as he cantered away.

Zoe thought about Pin as she, Jade, Gaby, and Becky rode along the shady road leading back toward Bright Field Stables. It had taken Pin a while to accept his role as duke.

At least he never had a problem with it to help his friends, Zoe thought with a smile. *But if I know Pin, he'll never be like those stuffy old dukes in most of the portraits . . .*

"So," Becky said abruptly, breaking the comfortable silence. "I was just wondering—should I start wearing more makeup, do you think?"

Zoe blinked in surprise, then turned in the saddle to stare at Becky, who was riding between the other girls. Jade and Gaby did the same.

"Makeup? Why?" Jade asked.

Becky shrugged, not quite meeting her friends' eyes.

"Oh, no reason," she said. "It's just I have a boyfriend now, and he's a bit older, and, well . . ."

"Becky!" Zoe exclaimed, pulling Raven to an abrupt halt. "You can't change yourself for a boy!"

"Especially not for Alex," Gaby said, chuckling.

"Right," Jade agreed, stopping Major as well. "Besides, Alex doesn't seem the type of boy who cares about makeup and that sort of thing."

"Well, I wouldn't have thought so, either." Becky sighed and pulled absently at Bob's reins—he'd drifted to a stop along with the other horses and was already reaching out for a tasty-looking leaf along the trail. "But lately it's as if he doesn't care about interesting stuff anymore—like ghost dogs, and the vlog, and all sorts of things I thought he loved as much as I do." Becky shot her friends a sidelong glance. "And if he's hanging out with Susie now . . ."

"Stop!" Zoe held up her hand like a traffic cop. "Don't even think that. Okay, maybe he has been acting kind of weird the past couple of days. You shouldn't jump to conclusions."

Gaby nodded. "You should talk to him if you're worried."

"Good idea," Zoe said. "But remember, whatever's going on with him, you can't change other people. Only the way you react to them." At her friends' surprised look, she grinned. "What? It's something my mom learned in yoga class. She was always saying it when Rosie and I would get in fights back home."

"Yoga Zoe is right, you know," Jade told Becky. "Talk to Alex—it's probably nothing. But if it is something, you know Pony Squad is here for you."

"Always," Zoe added with a firm nod.

"For sure," chorused Gaby.

"Sisters before misters, remember?" Jade said.

Becky cracked a small smile. "Ponies before phonies," she echoed, holding out one hand.

Zoe put a hand on top of Becky's and Gaby put her hand on top of Zoe's. Then Jade added her own hand to the pile.

"Pony Squad!" they all shouted, throwing their hands up at the same time.

Zoe gave Raven a small nudge with her heels to set him walking again. She was a little worried about Becky—what if Alex really was interested in Susie? But she tried not to worry about it. Whatever happened, they'd help Becky through it. Pony Squad was cool like that. They had a special bond that couldn't be broken— not by boy trouble, not by disagreements, and not even by misunderstandings.

"But speaking of sisters before misters, my bladder is thinking of toilet stops before friendship talks," Gaby said, smiling. "I gotta dash. I'll catch you all later!"

Becky, Jade, and Zoe wished good-bye to Gaby. Gaby . . . that reminded Zoe.

"Listen, you guys." She turned in the saddle to give her friends a serious look. "I'm really glad you didn't hold a grudge about that truth earlier. But can I tell you the rest of the reason why I chose Gaby?"

"Sure, I guess so," Jade said.

Becky nodded. "You don't have to, though, really," she said. "We already forgave you, remember?"

"I do." Zoe smiled at her. "But I don't want you two to think I trust Gaby more than you. It's just　" She gave Raven a rub on the withers, trying to figure out how to say what she wanted to say. "Well, you know I had a special bond with Raven from the start, right?"

"Right," Becky said. "Sort of like mine with Bob. Hey! Bob, stop trying to eat your reins!"

Jade laughed. "Yeah, nobody gets Bob like you do, Becky. And nobody could have tamed Raven like Zoe."

"Thanks." Zoe smiled briefly. "The thing is, you, Jade, have Major, and you, Becky, have Bob. Gaby had to let Ariel return to the wild. And it's still hurting her."

"I never thought about it that way," said Jade.

"That's the thing," Zoe said. "Gaby might be a tough cookie to love, but she'd do anything for horses."

Becky and Jade traded a look and nodded. "Makes sense," Becky said.

Zoe smiled down at her horse, suddenly overwhelmed by how lucky she was to have him—and her friends. "I know I can always count on you guys. And the thing is, you both *know* that I know that. But Gaby? Well, maybe she isn't always quite as certain about stuff like that. And she deserves to be."

"Oh!" Jade's eyes went wide. "I think I see what you're saying."

"Not me," Becky said. "What are you saying, Zoe?"

"I'm saying Gaby hasn't had many friends in her life," Zoe said. "It's not easy for her to trust people, you know? She's getting better, but I think it would mean a lot to her if I did ask her to take care of Raven. More than it would to you guys, maybe."

"Oh." Becky frowned slightly. "I think I get it. But Gaby's part of Pony Squad now—she should know we've got her back."

"Yeah, she should. I guess this silly Truth or Dare game just made me think of stuff like that—but I need to stop now, because it's making my head hurt!" Zoe said with a laugh.

"Silly game?" Becky said, sounding insulted. Just then her phone pinged. She pulled it out and glanced at it. "Just an update on the vlog's views," she told Zoe and Jade. "My followers don't think the Truth or Dare game is silly—we're still getting tons of hits! People especially seem to love the town hall video."

Jade grimaced. "Too bad that one got Heather grounded," she commented. "Becky, I know you're having fun with this Truth or Dare thing, but isn't it maybe time to do as Pin asked and end the game?"

"Yeah," Zoe said. "I think the Breakfast Club is getting carried away with their new fame. I mean, what if Winnie really had decided to ride Casper out along Moonlight Cliff?"

Jade shuddered. "I won't get close to the edge of that cliff even on my own two feet, let alone on horseback," she declared. "It's all loose gravel and slippery stone—it wouldn't take much of a stumble to cause a disaster!"

Becky looked a little disappointed, but she nodded. "I suppose you're right—the game's run its course. My fans will just have to deal with it."

Zoe smiled at her, glad they'd all had a chance to talk. "I'm sure they will." They'd just reached a wide, smooth part of the dirt road, so she gathered her reins. "Should we trot for a while?"

Zoe, Jade, and Becky were back at the yard untacking their horses when the Breakfast Club raced in.

"Hey!" Zoe called to them. "Come over here, okay? We need to talk to you." She shot Becky a meaningful look.

Becky made a face. But then she turned toward the younger kids. "Listen, about Truth or Dare . . ." she told them.

"Do you know where Marcus is?" Aaron rubbed his hands together. "I have a perfect dare for him—to use Bob's drool as hair gel!"

Winnie laughed. "Perfect!"

"Ooh, that does sound . . ." Becky began. She cut herself off when Jade gave her a sharp nudge. "Er, I mean no more dares. Game's over."

"What?" Heather cried.

"No way!" Aaron sounded dismayed. "But we're getting mega hits!"

"Exactly," Becky said. "We've got to quit while we're ahead. Always leave 'em wanting more."

"That's right," Zoe said. "If we quit now, we're legends. If we keep going, we'd be old news before you know it."

Heather still looked disappointed. But Aaron nodded.

"I guess that's true," he said. "It's like making too many sequels to a popular movie. The later ones are never as good."

"Right. So we're all done with dares, then," Jade said.

Heather sighed. "I guess so."

"Yeah," Aaron agreed sadly.

Zoe glanced at Winnie. She was staring at the ground not saying anything, which Zoe decided to take as agreement. Ever since backing out of that crazy dare about riding along the cliff, Winnie hadn't seemed quite as enthusiastic as the other two, anyway.

"Good," Zoe said. "Where's everybody else? We should tell them about this, too."

"Marcus is in the office with Mia, I think," Aaron said.

"What about Alex? Is he around?" Becky asked.

Heather shrugged. "Haven't seen him lately. Or Gaby or Susie, either."

Zoe traded a quick, worried look with Jade. Alex and Susie were missing again—coincidence? Or not?

"Let's go tell Marcus and Mia, anyhow," Jade suggested.

In the office, Mia was sitting on a stool fiddling with her boots while Marcus went through some papers at the desk. They both nodded when Becky told them about the game ending.

"Good riddance," Mia said. "Those kids were really getting carried away."

"We want to tell Alex and Susie, too," Becky said. "Have you seen them?"

"Don't forget Gaby," Jade spoke up.

"Gaby's with Scout, I think," Marcus said. "As for the other two, no idea."

Mia glanced up from her boot. "I saw them a while ago," she said. "I was looking for Susie—she promised to help clean my bridle."

Zoe rolled her eyes when Mia wasn't looking. Whenever Mia asked Susie to help her with something, Susie somehow always seemed to end up doing all the work herself. But she forgot about that at Mia's next words.

"I heard hoof beats," Mia said. "So I went out toward the arena just in time to see her and Alex riding off across the field." She frowned, looking annoyed. "I shouted after them, but they didn't even turn around."

Zoe glanced at Becky, whose face looked anxious. "Pony Squad," Becky whispered, just loud enough for Zoe and Jade to hear. Then she straightened up. "Which direction were they going, Mia?" she asked. "Because I need to have a talk with Alex. Right now."

A few minutes later, the horses were saddled again and Pony Squad was riding out past the arena. "Are you sure you want to do this, Becky?" Jade asked.

"I'm sure." Becky's voice was determined, even though her eyes still looked nervous. "If he's going to sneak around, I'm going to call him on it!"

Just then Gaby appeared around the corner. "Hey! Where are you going?" she called.

"To confront a sneaky boy," Zoe called back.

"Yeah—Alex!" Becky added. "He keeps sneaking off with Susie and I want to know why." She squared her shoulders. "I *deserve* to know why!"

"Ah, got it." Gaby gave a quick nod. "Don't go too fast, okay? I'll grab Jet and catch up before you hit the woods."

Soon the four of them were cantering across the moors. The grass was dry after a week without rain, and Gaby pointed out a recent track of broken grass stems leading off toward the sea.

"Good eye, Gaby." Becky sounded impressed. "That has to be them!"

They turned slightly to follow the track. "What are you going to do when you find them?" Gaby asked Becky.

Becky shrugged. "Not sure," she said. "I suppose I'll figure it out."

"With a little help from your friends," Zoe said.

A ping rang out. It was Becky's phone. When she checked it, she looked surprised. "It's from Alex!" she said.

"What does that sneaky rat have to say for himself?" Jade asked.

Becky was scanning the text. "Oh! He says he thinks he figured out the clue from the old book," she said. "He thinks the island's heart is that steep hill near here—you know, the one with the funny-shaped ridge on top. Come to think of it, it does look sort of like the top of a heart . . ." For a second she looked excited. "He's a genius! That's got to be it! It's pretty close to Moonlight Cliff, too, which makes sense with what Pin told us along with the other part of the clue . . ."

"'In full view of moonlight,'" Jade quoted.

"Right. He says if I want to check it out, he'll meet me in that little grove of lilacs nearby." Becky smiled. "And here I thought he wasn't interested in my treasure hunt!"

"Okay, but why'd he go hunting for your treasure with Susie of all people?" Gaby sounded skeptical.

Zoe shrugged. "One way to find out. Come on, Raven—we're going to the heart of the island!"

She brought her horse to a canter, and the others followed. They raced across the moor and up a steep slope. From the top, gentle hills rolled down toward the cliffs overlooking the beach. It was one of the prettiest views on the island, but Zoe and her friends didn't stop to enjoy it.

"There's the grove of lilacs," Zoe called over her shoulder. "Come on, we're almost there!"

"Lucky we were so close," Jade said breathlessly.

They cantered down the slope and across a meadow brimming with wildflowers. In the middle of the meadow stood a grove of large shrubs covered in purple flowers—buddleia, better known around the island as lilacs.

As they got closer, Zoe saw two horses tethered on the far side of the flowering shrubs. "There's Atilla and Darcy," she called.

"That means Alex and Susie are both here," Gaby said grimly.

Zoe slowed Raven to a trot. The grove of flowering shrubs was just ahead now. She stopped her horse and jumped down.

"Hello?" she called, leaving Raven grazing on the lush grass with Alex's and Susie's horses. "Alex? Anybody home?"

Alex's head popped into view over the top of the nearest buddleia. "Zoe!" he blurted out. "Uh—what are you doing here?"

"We're all here, actually," Jade said. She, Becky, and Gaby had dismounted by now, too.

"Right, and we want to know what's going on." Gaby pushed her way through the graceful branches of the flowering shrubs.

Zoe followed—and gasped at what she saw. In a little clearing right in the middle of the lush purple shrubs, a brightly colored blanket was spread on the grass, topped with platters of fruit and cheese, a pitcher of lemonade, a bowl of cookies, and a pretty scented candle. And kneeling at the edge of the picnic blanket was Susie.

"Aha—I knew there was something funny going on!" Zoe cried, spinning to point an accusing finger at Alex. "How could you do this to Becky? How dare you take another girl on a romantic picnic behind her back?"

*W*hat? No!" Alex exclaimed.

"No, no, no!" Susie added, looking alarmed. "How'd you get here so fast, anyway?"

"Yeah, we thought it would take you a good half hour to get all the way out here," Alex told Becky. "So Susie would have time to skedaddle before you arrived."

"And we definitely weren't expecting you to bring the whole Pony Squad with you," Susie added.

Zoe held up both hands, totally confused. "Wait—what's going on? Is this a secret romantic picnic or not?"

"Of course it is!" Susie put her hands on her hips. "For Alex and Becky!"

Alex smiled weakly at Becky. "Surprise!"

Becky gasped. "Wait—you mean you planned

this . . . for me?" she cried. "But this is only my most favorite romantic spot on the island!"

"I know." Alex grinned at her. "You told me when we rode through here last week."

"Yes, but Alex, well, you know . . ." Susie paused long enough to roll her eyes. "He wasn't sure what to do with the information. That's where I came in."

"Yeah," Alex said, grabbing Becky's hands and squeezing them. "I wanted to do something special together. Susie helped me put this picnic in motion—we've been planning it all week."

Zoe's eyes widened. She traded a slightly guilty look with Jade and Gaby. This explained a lot . . .

"Um, you guys weren't quite as stealthy as you probably intended," Jade said.

"Definitely not," Gaby agreed.

Becky was smiling up at Alex, still holding both his hands tightly in her own. "Oh well, no harm done," she said. "Ooh, and look—you got my favorite cookies from that place on the pier!"

"Only the best for the world's best girlfriend," Alex replied, leaning down to plant a kiss on her forehead.

"Aww." Zoe grinned. "Come on, you guys, maybe we should leave them to it."

"Thanks, guys—but wait!" Suddenly, Becky stood up very straight. "Alex, I think you're right about the spot where the treasure is hidden. It makes perfect sense!"

"Oh, yeah." Alex shrugged. "Susie helped me figure that out, too. She said I needed a proper excuse to get you to rush out here straightaway."

Susie glanced up from brushing a stray leaf off the picnic blanket. "It was obvious, really," she said. "Heart of the island—this place lies right beneath the shadow of that heart-shaped ridge at certain times of the day; plus, it's super romantic because of the flowers and whatnot. And you can hear the sea from here, and look—" She stepped to the far edge of the grove and parted the lush branches. "See? Perfect view of Moonlight Cliff."

"'In full view of moonlight,'" Jade recited. "'Where he could hear the voice of the sea 'neath the shadow of the island's heart.'"

"Exactly." Susie shrugged. "Can't see why you didn't figure it out already."

Zoe couldn't help being impressed. Susie spent so much time tagging along after Mia that it was easy to forget she was her own person—and a smart one, too, judging by the way she'd just solved a decades-old mystery!

"Go on and enjoy your picnic," Jade told Becky. "We can come back and look for the treasure tomorrow."

"What? No!" Becky cried.

Alex nodded. "Everyone grab a cookie or something," he said, scooping up a handful of grapes himself. "We'll need sustenance if we end up having to dig to find that treasure! Remember Valentine's Day?"

"Are you kidding me?" Susie looked slightly annoyed. "After all the work we put into this picnic, the least you could do is have it!"

"Oh." Becky stopped short and glanced at Alex. "Um, I know you did go to a lot of trouble, so if you want to have our picnic first . . ."

Alex laughed. "Are you kidding? We can't sit here sipping lemonade when there's a duke's long-lost treasure to be found!"

Zoe laughed, too. Becky and Alex really were the perfect couple!

"Come on," she said, scooping up a couple of cookies. "Let's go find the duke's greatest treasure!"

"There's a folding shovel in my saddlebag," Becky said.

"I'll get it," Jade offered, dashing off in the direction of the horses.

"Fine, whatever." Susie sighed. "I suppose I'll stay here

and make sure a bird doesn't fly off with all the cookies . . ."

Leaving Susie fussing over the picnic, the rest of the group followed Becky out the far side of the grove. Moonlight Cliff lay ahead. The sun was just beginning to dip toward the horizon, turning the rocky scree at the drop-off pink and silver.

"I was thinking it should be just here." Alex stepped forward, squinting up toward the heart-shaped top of the hill nearby. "This spot would be shadowed in the morning, right?"

"Okay." Becky glanced around. "So if you were a duke, where would you bury your most valuable treasure?"

Just then Jade caught up, gripping the folding shovel in one hand. "Did you figure it out?" she asked breathlessly.

Gaby was staring toward Moonlight Cliff, not seeming especially interested in the treasure hunt. "It's odd that this spot is so important, isn't it?" she mused.

Zoe shrugged. "Not really. Pin told us this was one of Peter the Young's favorite spots. And it is one of the nicest areas of the island. I mean, it's where Becky and Alex decided to have their romantic picnic, right?"

"Yes, and we ride through here all the time," Jade added. "Lots of people come here for the views and the flowers and whatnot."

Becky had been examining the ground nearby. She looked up. "Can we focus, people? We need to find the treasure!"

Gaby finally turned away from the cliff. She squinted up at the heart-shaped ridge, then glanced around. "How about here?" she suggested, stepping over and tapping something with her boot. "Under this weird rock that doesn't look as if it belongs here."

"You're right." Jade bent to peer at the rock. "This rock is smooth, like the ones in riverbeds or down by the sea. It didn't get here by itself."

Becky gasped. "That's got to be it! Come on—help me dig!"

She grabbed the shovel and went to work. Zoe found a stout stick and started chipping at the ground, while the others did their best with rocks or their hands.

After a moment, there was a clink. "I hit something!" Becky cried.

"It could just be a rock," Gaby said.

But Alex flung himself onto the ground beside Becky, pulling aside the loose dirt with his hands. "It's not a rock," he exclaimed. "I think it's a metal box!"

Another few minutes of work unearthed the rest of the box. Becky knelt and pulled it loose, wiping the dirt from its dented sides.

"The treasure," she said breathlessly. "It has to be!"

Jade leaned closer, pointing to a symbol carved in the lid. "Look—that's Pin's family crest," she said. "This could actually be it!"

"Go ahead and open it, Becky," Zoe urged, feeling excited now, too. Were they really about to reveal some fabulous long-lost treasure? She wished Pin was here— but since he wasn't, she pulled out her phone and turned on the video camera.

"Oh! Good idea, Zoe!" Becky told her. "I was so excited I almost forgot to film this super-important moment!"

Zoe focused on the box as Becky picked the dirt off the latch. "Is it locked?" Jade asked.

"No, just latched shut. Okay, here goes . . ." Becky said.

She flipped open the lid. For a second, nobody said anything.

"Where's the treasure?" Gaby asked at last. "It's just an empty box."

"Not totally empty." Alex carefully lifted out the two items inside the box—a folded scrap of parchment and a small, blue collar.

Becky grabbed the parchment and unfolded it carefully. "Whoa, the writing looks really old," she said. "I can hardly read it."

Jade leaned over her shoulder. "It's hard to make out," she said. "But I think it says something about a memento of a most treasured friend, er . . ." She squinted. "Does that say, uh . . . Marshmallow the dog?"

Gaby barked out a laugh. "Hang on. The treasure is a collar from the duke's pet dog?"

"Looks that way." Zoe grinned, though it faded slightly when she noticed Becky's crestfallen expression.

Jade marveled over the collar. "Marshmallow," she said. "I wonder if he looked like Puffball! Maybe Marshmallow is one of Puffball's ancestors, just like Peter the Young is Pin's. That would be pretty neat."

Everyone agreed. Everyone, that is, except Becky. She looked a little sad.

"Hey," Zoe said, nudging her friend. "Don't look so glum. Anybody can find some boring old gold coins or brooches or whatever. But this? It's one of a kind!"

"Right!" Jade chimed in. "What a cool story—a duke with all the wealth in the world, and his most treasured possession is a reminder of his beloved pet. Tourists would love to hear the story of Peter the Young and Marshmallow."

"Sweet, really," Alex said with a nod.

"I bet Pin will love hearing the story," Zoe agreed. "Loving animals must run in his family. Maybe he can frame the note and the collar and display them in the castle!"

Becky brightened. "That's a fab idea!" she said. "And how many castles can say they have something like that on display?" She smiled, looking thrilled. "This is actually the coolest treasure ever!"

Gaby chuckled. "If you say so."

"I do!" Becky told her. "I'll have to check those old books we found—maybe there's a picture of Marshmallow in there!"

Still talking about their find, the whole group wandered back into the buddleia grove, where Susie was just finishing packing up the picnic. "It'll be getting dark soon," she said. "I figured you guys can try this again another day." Noticing the box under Becky's arm, she added, "Oh! Did you find the treasure?"

Zoe, Becky, and Jade traded a grin. "We did," Jade told Susie. "And you'll never believe what it is . . ."

It took a few more minutes to tell Susie about their discovery and then help her finish packing up. Finally, Zoe squinted up at the sun, which was sinking toward the horizon in earnest now.

"We'd better get going," she said. "Grandpa is expecting me for dinner."

"Okay." Becky stood on tiptoes to give Alex a kiss on the cheek. "Thanks for the most romantic picnic ever!" Seeing Susie watching, she stepped over and kissed her on the cheek, too. "And thanks for helping him."

"You're welcome." Susie wiped her cheek, then smiled. "It was certainly . . . interesting."

Gaby laughed. "Come on, let's go."

They all pushed their way back out of the grove. Up ahead, the horses were still grazing where they'd left them. But now there were three ponies standing in front of the group—Casper, Paolo, and Princess. Aaron was mounted on Paolo, while Heather was holding the other two. Both kids looked scared.

"What in the world are you doing here?" Jade hurried forward and glanced around. "Is Winnie with you?"

Zoe gasped as she noticed something else. "Hey! Where'd Raven go?"

"Winnie talked us into following you out here," Heather said. "She said she was just curious about where you guys were going."

Aaron gulped. "Yeah. But she really wanted to prove she wasn't a chicken after all. You know, I offered her the truth, but she kept saying that Bright Fields kids are brave, so she took a dare . . ."

"What do you mean?" Gaby asked.

The two younger kids traded a look. "She grabbed Raven," Aaron said. "She's going to ride him along Moonlight Cliff!"

*W*hat?" For a second, Zoe felt as if her heart had stopped entirely. Then it started up again, but at double speed. "She took *Raven*?"

Heather nodded. "Er, or tried to. She said riding Casper there would be too easy," she said. "She wanted to prove she was as brave as anyone. She's been feeling really left out lately, if you couldn't tell."

"We have to stop her!" Jade exclaimed. "If Raven takes one wrong step . . ."

"I don't want to think about that," Becky gulped.

Zoe was already racing toward Darcy. Susie's mare let out a surprised snort when Zoe vaulted onto her back, strapping on her helmet as she did. "Hi-yah!" Zoe said, gently nudging Darcy into a gallop.

"Hey!" Susie called.

"Zoe, wait up!" Gaby added.

But Zoe didn't slow down or look back. Darcy raced across the meadow, veering around the buddleia grove. Now Zoe could see Moonlight Cliff right ahead—and Raven, rearing wildly on the edge!

"Raven!" she yelled, though she was still too far away for him to hear her. "Stop—no!"

Zoe urged Darcy on even faster. Finally, they had almost reached the cliff. Zoe pulled up, flinging herself off before the mare had come to a full stop.

"Raven!" she cried, taking a few steps forward. "Please, you have to calm down!"

Raven responded by tossing his head, which brought a squeak of terror from Winnie, who was holding on as tight as she could. "Whoa!" Winnie's thin voice came.

"Raven!" Zoe called again.

This time the horse turned slightly to look at her—which caused one hind hoof to skid and lurch down over the edge of the cliff. Raven tossed his head and let out a panicked neigh, scrabbling for a second before catching himself.

The breath caught in Zoe's throat. That had been close!

Behind her, a couple of other horses skidded to a halt. "Careful, Zoe," Jade called. "Don't get too close!"

"Yeah—looks like he's panicking," Gaby added.

Zoe didn't bother glancing back at her friends. She kept her gaze trained on Raven, who pranced in place for a moment, tossed his head, and reared again. Gaby was right—he wasn't thinking right now, just reacting. Zoe had seen him this way before. But never in such a precarious spot!

"Help!" Winnie looked like she was about to slide off. "He isn't listening to me!"

Zoe gulped. "Just hang on!" she called, her heart squeezing. Winnie looked so young—for a second Zoe flashed to her little sister, Rosie, who was around the same age.

Then she shook her head. She had to focus! When Raven got like this, there was only one thing that could bring him out of it—namely, Zoe herself.

"Raven!" she called, trying to keep her voice as calm as possible. She took a step forward, holding out her hands. "Raven, it's me!"

Behind her, she could hear that the rest of the group had arrived. "Winnie, are you okay?" Heather called.

"No!" Winnie squeaked out. "Help me!"

"I'm coming, Winnie," Zoe called. "Just try not to panic, okay? And hold on tight."

She took another step closer. Her foot hit a stone,

which skittered forward and bounced away over the cliff's edge. Raven heard it, spun, and snorted.

"Zoe!" Susie sounded anxious. "You can't go any closer, it isn't safe!"

Zoe ignored her. "Easy, boy," she crooned, focusing all her energy on the horse in front of her. "Easy. It's me, okay? Just settle down . . ."

She took another step forward. "Zoe, no!" Jade cried. "Don't get any closer to the edge!"

"Let her go," Gaby said. "She knows what she's doing."

Zoe shot Gaby a brief, grateful glance. Alex was standing with the horses, who were several yards back from the cliff. The rest of Zoe's friends had drifted closer to watch. Most of them looked terrified. But Gaby was smiling.

"You can do it, Zoe," she called. "Remember—he'll do anything for you. You just have to remind him."

Zoe nodded and turned to face her horse again. She took a deep breath. "Raven," she called, just as he reared again. "Raven, it's me . . ."

She kept talking, not even sure what she was saying. When she saw his ear tilt in her direction, she took a step forward. Then another.

"I'm here, boy," she said. "I've got you. Take it easy . . ."

Raven shifted his weight, which sent a few rocks clattering over the edge of the cliff. Winnie let out another squeak of terror.

But Zoe kept her gaze trained on her horse—her beautiful, special, wonderfully unpredictable horse. Her whole mind and soul reached out to him, reminding him of their one-of-a-kind, unbreakable bond.

"Raven," she murmured, reaching up toward his face.

He tossed his head. But then he lowered it, snuffling at her.

She stroked his cheeks, still talking softly to him. Trusting him. Loving him.

"Grab him, Zoe!" Alex called. "You've got him!"

Zoe was tempted to do just that. But any sudden move could set him off again. Besides, she had to let him know that she trusted him to do the right thing.

"Come on, Raven," Zoe said, hooking one hand loosely around the cheek piece of his bridle and giving a gentle tug. "Ready to get out of here?"

He pulled back. For a second she thought he might yank his head free, rear again, maybe skitter backward . . .

But he didn't do any of those things. Letting out a deep sigh, he lowered his head again—and took a step toward her. Winnie relaxed. She finally got hold of Raven enough that she was feeling good.

"Good boy," Zoe crooned, moving back, away from the cliff. "Just a little farther . . ."

This time there was no hesitation. Raven followed her, step by step, until they were back to the others.

Becky and Jade leaped forward to envelop Zoe in a hug. At the same time, Gaby grabbed Raven's reins, while Alex and Susie helped Winnie get out of the saddle.

"Oh my Bob, Zoe, that was so scary!" Becky exclaimed, squeezing so tightly that Zoe could hardly breathe. "But you did it!"

"Raven did it," Zoe said, pulling back and glancing at the horse, who was standing calmly beside Gaby. "He didn't want to hurt anyone. He knew how to do the right thing. I just had to remind him."

The next day, Zoe, Jade, and Becky watched as Pin carefully hung a shadow box on the wall of a portrait-lined castle corridor. Displayed inside were the collar and parchment note they'd found the afternoon before.

"There," Pin said, stepping back. "How's it look?"

"Perfect!" Becky said as she filmed the whole thing on her phone.

"I guess liking Moonlight Cliff isn't the only thing

that runs in this particular branch of the royal family," Jade commented. "Being crazy about animals does, too. We have Peter the Young and his ghost dog."

Zoe smiled. "And Pin and horses."

Pin raised an eyebrow. "Hmm, I suppose you have a point at that," he agreed, glancing at the framed collar.

"In any case, I'm sure Peter the Young would be happy to have his canine friend honored like this," Jade said.

"Becky's followers are going to love it, too," Zoe added. "All—what is it? Eighty gazillion of them?"

Becky lowered her camera. "Actually, we lost a few when I announced that Truth or Dare game was over," she said sadly. "I'm back down to, um . . ." She scrolled through her phone for a moment, then sighed. "Twenty-seven. Wow, that's even lower than last time I checked."

Jade looked worried. "You're not thinking of starting up the game again?"

"No!" Zoe blurted out. "Please don't."

"Really? But I never got a turn," Pin said.

All three girls turned to stare at him in surprise. "You actually wanted to play Truth or Dare?" Zoe exclaimed.

Pin laughed. "Kidding," he said. "That game sounded crazy."

"It was." Zoe glanced at Becky. "I mean, it almost broke up Pony Squad!"

"No way." Jade reached over and squeezed her shoulder. "Okay, we were a little bit cross with you for a little while. But nothing can break up Pony Squad."

"No way!" Becky agreed.

Zoe smiled, happy to hear it. "Still," she said, wandering closer to examine the portrait of Peter the Young hanging next to the collar display. "You have to admit that game did cause some problems."

Becky shuddered. "Like Winnie and Raven, you mean?"

"Yeah." Pin frowned. "Though I did hear that Zoe has an *excellent* singing voice."

"Poor Winnie," Jade said. "She really feels terrible about what happened. She was only trying to prove she wasn't a chicken like Aaron said."

"That's what can happen when friends get too competitive with one another, I guess," Zoe said, thinking about herself and Gaby. They had competed hard to win that spot on the UK under 18 team   had it affected their friendship? She wasn't sure. But she hoped not.

"In any case, she apologizes every time she sees any of us now," Jade told Pin. "I doubt she'll make that sort of mistake again."

Just then the door at the end of the corridor opened. A flash of white fur burst toward them, barking excitedly.

"Sorry!" Bea called, hurrying into the corridor. "I was

looking to take him outside, but I opened the wrong door."

"Don't worry." Pin smiled at her. "Happens to me all the time in this huge old place."

"Hi, Puffball!" Becky greeted the little white dog.

Puffball barked at her, then leaped forward, jumping up against the stone wall trying to reach the shadow box.

"Naughty thing!" Bea exclaimed, hurrying to grab the pup. "That's not a toy."

"It's okay, Puffball." Jade kneeled and ruffled the fluffy puppy's white fur. "We're excited about the treasure, too."

Zoe's gaze shifted to a portrait a little farther down the wall—Peter the Young. Did the ghost of his loyal pup really haunt this island? Sure, the sightings in the wood nearby had turned out to be a very live pup instead. But who knew what was out there, really?

"Come on, Zoe," Becky said, breaking into her thoughts.

"Huh?" Zoe turned to look at her friends.

"We just offered to take Puffball for a walk," Jade said. "Are you coming?"

"Oh! Sure." Zoe trailed behind her friends as they headed for the door. She stepped outside, breathing in the scents of grass, moss, old stone, fresh air, and horses— plus a tiny hint of dry leaves indicating that autumn would be arriving soon. Then she glanced over at Raven, who was grazing nearby with Elvis, Major, and Bob. Had it only been a little over a year ago that he'd come into her life? Along with Pony Squad, and Pin, and Gaby, and the rest of the Bright Fields gang . . . It was hard to imagine her life without any of them. For one thing, she never would have found herself digging for a duke's treasure anywhere else, with anyone else. Or rescuing someone from the edge of a cliff overlooking the sea. Or competing for the Junior team, or cleaning a duke's castle, or tracking ghosts through a spooky wood, or any of the other adventures she'd had since coming to this island, a million miles from her old life in LA.

Pin leaned closer. "Penny for your thoughts," he said softly. "You look very far away all of a sudden."

"Oh, I was just thinking how lucky I am." Zoe smiled up at him.

After the drama on Moonlight Cliff, Zoe knew one thing for certain. Whether she went back to California or stayed here on the island, she would take Raven with her. Raven didn't just need a home, he needed her.

free REIN

The Steeplechase Secret

Discover more about Zoe, Raven, and Bright
Field Stables in *The Steeplechase Secret*

An Island Visitor

Zoe breathed in the salty sea air and felt the breeze against her face. On impulse, she tugged off her boots and socks and dug her toes into the sand. She faced the ocean, curly wisps of hair fluttering in the wind. She closed her hazel eyes to feel the sun on her face, and—*BAM*!

"Raven!" Zoe yelped, stumbling forward. "Way to ruin the moment!" Raven, who had just playfully head butted Zoe during her almost-perfect Zen moment, tossed his head in the air with a neigh. Zoe laughed and reached her arm around the beautiful black horse's neck. She took a deep breath and realized that *this* was the moment she had been working for—fighting for—ever since she had arrived on this small English island a couple of months earlier. Zoe leaned into Raven, giving him a hug. Raven snorted and dropped his coal-black head to rest on Zoe's shoulder.

"Hey, boy," she whispered into his tangled mane. "Isn't it great? No training. No Junior Nationals. No obligation to former owners who want you to win every competition." Zoe was referring to Raven's previous owner. Raven had been through a lot in his life: stolen as a foal and then shipwrecked, washing up on an island— the very island that was now their home. After that, he'd been horse-napped! But now he belonged to Zoe, and she belonged to him. It was the one thing of which Zoe was certain.

Maybe Raven hadn't minded the pressure of all the competitions, but Zoe was thrilled that life was back to normal—well, the new normal. Her old normal life was thousands of miles away, across a continent and an ocean, in Los Angeles, California. That's where she had lived her whole life until her mom decided to bring Zoe and her little sister, Rosie, to the island to visit their grandfather.

Zoe's mom had grown up on the island. She was used to being separated from the rest of the world, in a big, old stone house with a gorgeous garden and yard, where the only social life was at the local riding stables, Bright Fields. But surprisingly, Zoe was getting used to it, too.

Now her world revolved around Raven and Bright Fields. She'd made *horse-some* friends in Jade and Becky—together, they were Pony Squad! She'd also made a formidable frenemy in Mia, and she'd even had a couple of attempts at a proper boyfriend. First with Marcus, and then there was Pin. If things kept going well when Pin came back from Vienna, maybe they'd actually be able to make it "official" between them once and for all. Man, a lot had happened in a few months!

Zoe could hardly believe that her mom and Rosie had remained on the island just so Zoe could stay with Raven. "You really turned our world upside down, didn't you?" she said to him. As she thought about her old life, she gazed out at the ocean. A long, flat ferryboat caught her eye. Zoe hadn't seen any ferries dock at this side of the island. The ferries to the mainland usually came in at the pier, where there was an ice cream parlor and a couple of other attractions.

Zoe clucked to Raven and led him to the other side of the beach. "Let's get a better look," she said. Why would the boat be docking there? A little part of her told her she should just leave it alone. After all the drama with Raven and the horse stealers, she had promised her mom—and her dad, via Skype—that she would lie low and focus on her own responsibilities, like schoolwork—and Raven, of course. Still, Zoe could not contain her curiosity. On closer inspection, she could see a large SUV, a two-horse trailer, a bunch of building supplies like lumber and bags of sand, and many bales of hay and bags of grain.

"Looks pretty tasty, right?" Zoe said, patting Raven's neck, but she kept her eyes on the boat.

Just then, a boy walked to the bow and leaned over the railing. He wore a V-neck sweater with a crisp collared shirt and looked a couple of years older than Zoe. Soon, a man in a suit came up behind the boy and put a hand on his shoulder. Zoe wondered where they were headed. The island had several stables. What were the chances that they were bound for Bright Fields?

"We really should be getting back," Zoe said, as much to herself as to Raven. "Let's go, boy." But as she turned to go, Raven stayed put, still eyeing the ferry. He snorted.

"I know," Zoe said. "Something feels weird about it to me, too, but I'm sure it's nothing." Zoe looked at her horse, who did not seem convinced. "Not everything is a conspiracy!" she insisted, sounding a lot like her mom.

Raven sighed and dropped his head. When Zoe lightly jangled the reins and rubbed his ear, he followed. She trudged back to where she'd discarded her footwear. "Ugh! Sand in the socks is not a good feeling with boots on," she mumbled to herself. Raven whinnied as if to laugh at her. "I know, I know. Serves me right."

By the time Zoe made it back to Bright Fields, the excess sand was bugging her so much that she let her feet dangle out of the stirrups.

"If you would stay *on* the horse, where you belong, these things wouldn't happen to you, Zoe," Mia declared. "You keep forgetting that Raven and you are horse and rider. It's not like you're mates."

Zoe scowled. "Speak for yourself. You and Firefly may have that relationship, but Raven and I have a special bond," Zoe said, patting Raven's neck.

Still in the saddle, she pulled off her boot and turned it over. Just as the sand started to spill out, Raven snorted and blew a cloud of sand grains right in Mia's face. Zoe tried (only a little) to contain her laughter, and Mia stomped off.

Zoe had come to learn that Mia could be a little less insufferable when she wanted to be—nice, even— *sometimes.* She'd still probably never stop making snarky comments or acting like she always knew best. But Mia had her reasons for being, well, Mia, and Zoe just had to keep reminding herself of that.

Jade and Becky were a far more welcome sight on Zoe's return to the stables. Pony Squad sat together in the tack room as Zoe cleaned the sand off her feet. "I got to see a super-sized ferry arrive and dock all the way over by the cove," she said to her friends. "That's kind of weird, right?"

Becky's expression grew serious. She tugged on her super-tight French braid, deep in thought. "Very weird," she agreed, always willing to consider the most unlikely explanations first. Becky was, after all, a firm believer in the so-called ghost pony who haunted the island. "Maybe it's a pirate boat! Or a boat full of *ghost* pirates! Or a gravy boat! Wait, that's not right . . ."

Jade, as usual, opted for a rational explanation instead. "Maybe the other pier was too crowded? It does get quite busy at this time of year." Just then, Mia waltzed into the tack room with Susie, her second in command, at her flank. In her hand Mia held a fancy cream-colored envelope embossed with a gold horseshoe.

"That ferry was just the first of many," she announced. She waved the envelope like an ornate fan. Zoe would never understand how Mia's poker-straight hair always looked salon fresh after hours at the stables. "A partnership from the mainland is investing in the old Grindlerock Racing Grounds. They're going to rehabilitate it and then sponsor a formal steeplechase event at the end of the month."

This news inspired the gasps of awe that Mia had hoped for—from everyone except Zoe.

"They're using that dock because it's better for oversized deliveries, like building equipment, trailers, and *top-ranked* European racehorses," Mia went on. She watched Zoe closely for her reaction, but Zoe didn't blink or even raise her eyebrows. "Isn't it thrilling?" Mia prompted.

"Oh, yes," Susie said on command. "Thrilling."

When Mia stared her down, Zoe finally commented. "Well, I might be thrilled, but you lost me at Grindlehock, and then you lost me again at steeplechase."

"It's *Grindlerock*," Mia corrected, "and it was once a stately racecourse that attracted tourists from the mainland every weekend of the competitive season. Of course, that was long before our time, but everyone knows it was lush and lovely."

"This is an island," Zoe stated. "We've ridden all over

the place. How is there a big, fancy racetrack here that I've never seen?"

"Well," Mia replied, "Ireland and Australia are islands, too. Have you explored every square kilometer of those islands as well?"

"O-kay," Zoe replied. Mia had a point. The island did have all kinds of nooks and crannies that Zoe hadn't explored. This place was full of surprises! "But what are you so excited about, Mia? It's just a racetrack. You were a show jumper last I knew."

"Oh, Zoe," Mia said. "You are so provincially American. Steeplechase is not your stateside version of racing. It's not like the Triple Crown or other straight gallop-to-the-finish races. Steeplechase is a race with jumps. It is a quintessentially British event."

"Because they wear hats?" Zoe asked hopefully. Was there anything more British than the elegant spectator hats that they wore to weddings and parades and other posh affairs?

"Yes, because they wear hats," Mia confirmed. "And there will be hats at the Grindlerock opening event as well. You will all need one since you'll want to come cheer for Firefly and me."

"Hats? I'll make you a hat," Becky offered. "I have a

bunch of old lampshades that I've been saving for a major crafting event—I knew they'd come in handy!"

"Um, no, thanks," Mia promptly replied.

"Wait. You're racing?" Jade asked Mia. "That sounds intense."

"Well, my dad met Mr. Cooke, the event promoter, on the mainland. They hit it off, of course. When Daddy told him about my performance at Junior Nationals, Mr. Cooke asked me to compete. This is the invitation." Mia paused and raised her eyebrows for effect. "I figure we need something to focus on now that Junior Nationals are over. Who's with me?" Mia immediately turned to Zoe.

"Um, no," Zoe answered. "Raven and I need some downtime. And training for a high-profile tourist attraction with hurdles and fancy hats is anything but that."

She and Raven needed a rest. Still, it was kind of exciting, knowing that the island would host a big event in just a few weeks.

"Why don't we ride out to this old track tomorrow and see it for ourselves?" Zoe tossed her chaps into her tack trunk. "The weather's supposed to be nice, and since we don't have to train, we could take a picnic and be gone all afternoon."

"Oh! I could bake something horse-some, like carrot-cake doughnuts," Becky suggested. "They're Bob's favorite. And mine." Bob was Becky's pony.

"That sounds delicious—and fun," Jade agreed.

"I know Raven could use more time exploring and less time in the ring practicing," Zoe said, loving her plan even more. "I could, too."

"An old racing track?" Becky said absentmindedly, not seeming to have heard a word Zoe just said. "Think of all the expectations and hope over the years. The adrenaline. The rivalries. The heartbreak." She went on with a faraway look in her eyes. "I'll bet there are at least three ghost ponies trapped in the race grounds. Or maybe ghost *jockeys*," Becky whispered. Jade and Zoe turned to her. "Oh, did I say that out loud?" Becky asked, biting her lower lip.

"You did," Jade responded, giving her best friend a knowing smile. "But we'll pretend you didn't." Becky had a habit of letting her imagination get away with her. Jade preferred to stick to the facts. "We're not going on a whole ghost pony quest tomorrow. It's just a jaunt. For fun," Jade insisted. "To celebrate not having to train for Junior Nationals anymore."

Becky gave an enthusiastic smile, her braid bobbing with each nod. "Absolutely," she said. But something told Zoe that ghost ponies—or other kinds of ghosts—were still running wild in Becky's mind.

This will just be an innocent little field trip, Zoe told herself. *There won't be anything strange or mysterious at all. Right?*

The Grindlerock Curse

After Zoe had picked Raven's hooves, brushed the sand from his fetlocks, and given him an apple just because she liked to spoil him, she headed home—to her new decidedly British home. With the broad-leafed ivy growing up the stone front, the old manor looked like something out of a book Zoe would have to read for Advanced English Literature. Surprisingly, her grandfather's house was rather charming and cozy inside.

She found her mom and ten-year-old sister in the kitchen. Her mother was making tacos—from scratch. The island market didn't stock any of the family's preferred dinner shortcuts, and, despite the fact that her mom was filling in as a part-time manager at Bright Fields, she still had an inordinate amount of time on her hands. Back in LA, she had always been busy, tackling twelve tasks at a time and volunteering for all kinds of worthy organizations. It was harder to do that on the island, especially since the Wi-Fi connection was not the most reliable. "Zoe!" her mom exclaimed, her smile extra bright. "How was your day?"

"You seem happy to see me," Zoe said, suspicious.

"She doesn't like the way I cut the tomatoes," Rosie said, scrunching up her mouth in a pout. Unlike her mom and sister, who let their tight curls naturally frame their faces, Rosie wore her hair straightened, with soft waves. "I don't know why I should have to cut them when I don't even like them."

"Don't be ridiculous," her mother said. "You like salsa, and that is approximately eighty-five percent tomatoes."

"Well, I must really like the other fifteen percent, because I detest tomatoes," Rosie insisted.

"Here, I'll help," Zoe said, washing her hands. "Your technique is awful." She walked over to the counter and playfully nudged Rosie out of the way.

"You should help, because if it weren't for you, we'd be back in LA, and we could go to any trendy restaurant or hole-in-the-wall cantina and eat like queens," Rosie said.

"Instead, we're here so you can bond with Raven. And we have to eat Mom's food."

"Hey," Zoe's mom objected.

"Come on, Rosie, quit pretending you don't have fun at the stables, too. Why didn't you come today and ride Prince?" Prince was one of Mia's old show ponies. Mia actually liked Rosie and was letting her ride him for lessons.

"If you must know, Prince called in. He needed some 'me time,'" Rosie said. "So I obliged. And did my nails." She waved her hands in front of Zoe.

"Oh, yet another shade of pink," Zoe said. "Is that Cotton Candy Confetti?"

"How'd you guess?" Rosie asked, admiring the shiny gloss for herself.

"It's a talent," Zoe replied, slicing the tomatoes into cubes. The truth was that Zoe had stepped on the bottle that Rosie had left on the patio on her way in, spilling the shocking pink color in a small puddle. "More importantly, I have news. There's going to be some kind of race. A horse race with hurdles. They're reopening an old track and hosting a big opening-day event that will bring in tourists from all over. It's going to be in a few weeks."

"Really? Are you kidding?" Rosie's face lit up. "It's about time we got some excitement around here. Nothing ever happens. Nothing ev-er."

"How can you say that?" Zoe's mom asked with a laugh. After all, they had only been living there for a few months and they had already encountered horse thieves, a smugglers' legacy that revealed the humble stable boy was the descendant of a wealthy duke, and an impulsive proposal by their grandfather to a fortune-teller. Personally, Zoe thought it had been a rather eventful stay.

"Well, a proper horse race is more my kind of event," Rosie admitted.

"There will be hats," Zoe said. Rosie eyed her uncertainly.

"Not hard hats for riding," Zoe confirmed. "Big, colorful hats for looking sophisticated, borderline ridiculous."

Rosie gasped. "Like at the royal weddings?"

"Exactly." Zoe was happy to see her sister really smile again.

"Now this is going to be good," Rosie insisted, shuffling out of the room in her heels. "No one else get on the Internet. No slowing down the Wi-Fi. I *have* to research. I need the perfect outfit. I only get one chance to select my debut spectator hat and choose the best accompanying ensemble. Three weeks is not much time for this kind of thing!"

Zoe and her mom locked eyes and tried not to laugh out loud. "At least she's excited about something," her mom said.

"I'm excited about this dinner," Zoe said. "It looks like it's going to be good."

"It had better be. I've been chopping for an hour!" her mom replied. "So, how did you hear about this upcoming race?"

"Mia had all the news, as usual. She was apparently invited to compete by the head organizer himself," Zoe said. "She was trying to get everyone else to do it, too."

"And?" her mom prompted.

"Are you kidding? I don't know the first thing about steeplechase races," Zoe said, popping a cherry tomato into her mouth.

"Well, I have to admit, I'm glad to hear you're taking it a bit easy for once," her mom said, eyeing her daughter carefully. "Maybe that's for the best. Trouble certainly has seemed to find you easily since we moved here."

The last thing Zoe wanted was her mom worrying about her again. It wasn't that long ago that her mom hadn't even wanted her riding at all. She'd finally come around, but who's to say she wouldn't change her mind again with all the crazy things that had happened lately? "Don't worry, Mom," Zoe said quickly. "I promise, no more drama for me. I'm staying out of it—the riskiest thing I have planned is a picnic tomorrow that involves eating something Becky usually bakes for Bob."

Her mom laughed and seemed to relax. She proceeded to tell Zoe that her great-aunt Zelda had competed at Grindlerock. "I'm certain we have a picture of her around here somewhere. She was my mum's sister. Anyway, it really was the thing to do back in the day, but then there were a number of freak accidents. After a string of them, rumors started about the course being cursed."

"Oh, come on," Zoe said, rolling her eyes. "What is it about this island and tall tales?"

Her mom shook her head. "No, really. People say it's one of the reasons that Grindlerock was finally shut down," she said. "I mean, this was all long before I was born, but I heard lots of stories."

"Of course you did. This place is full of stories," Zoe said with a smile. One of Zoe's favorite parts of being in England was finding out more about her mom's own childhood.